A Cruel Confession

THE OBSESSION DUET BOOK TWO

Vi Carter

Contents

Other Books by VI CARTER

Other Books by VI CARTER

<u>WILD IRISH SERIES</u>

FATHER (FREE)

VICIOUS #1

RECKLESS # 2

RUTHLESS #3

FEARLESS #4

HEARTLESS #5

<u>THE BOYNE CLUB</u>

DARK #1

DARKER # 2

DARKEST #3

PITCH BLACK #4

<u>THE OBSESSED DUET</u>

A DEADLY OBSESSION #1

A CRUEL CONFESSION #2

<u>YOUNG IRISH REBELS</u>

MAFIA PRINCE #1

MAFIA KING #2

MAFIA GAMES #3

MAFIA BOSS #4

<u>MURPHY'S MAFIA MADE MEN</u>

SINNER'S VOW #1

SAVAGE MARRIAGE #2

SCANDALOUS PLEDGE #3

CHAPTER ONE

LUCAS

Frustration claws at me as I take down another book. The writing is more faded this time. More rules about the members or disqualifying a member of the elite on moral grounds. I close the book on that. *They have no morals.*

My heritage, my life, surrounds me and the more I learn, the worse it gets. I had never cared for rules; they don't apply to me most of the time. All I ever wanted to do was bury my pain of losing my mother and make my father proud. Two things I failed at.

I push out the chair and stand. I'm searching for a needle in a haystack. I'm not even sure what I'm looking for. I run my hand across my face. My gaze darts to the red leather notepad. Someone left it there for me to find. I just wish whoever it was would tell me what they want me to know.

That voice of doubt in the back of my head reminds me it could be my father sending me on a goose chase. I leave the room.

My father is ordering the staff around as they move some of the furniture.

"Finally catching up on studying?" my father asks without looking at me.

"The meeting will be in thirty minutes. Be here."

I want to go and see Ella, but I nod. "I'll be there."

"You know I only want the best for you, son." My stomach twists. A part of me wants to make this right with him. I've always sought out his praise.

"Every choice I make is never easy. One day you'll understand." Why don't I believe him? I hope I never understand, because if I do, I'll be like him.

I leave and he doesn't stop me. I feel bare, as if I am going to war with only two small weapons and I'm not even sure how powerful they are. One, is that I could have the committee informed about Henry's sodomy, and two, I could bring up the rule about my father remarrying. If we can't get a nice woman, she won't pass these laws, but I don't have that kind of time. Each second is a second too long to have Ella stuck in a cell.

George is waiting for me when I step into the kitchen. My paranoia takes a leap into the vicinity that suggests he's tracking me.

"Master Lucas." He greets me with an incline of his head.

"Is that done?" I ask.

He nods.

"I need you to do something else for me."

"Anything." His eager words have me smiling. He might not be so eager when he hears my request.

"I need the key to the cell."

His eyes widen, and there's a moment of hesitation. I want to tell him it's fine. It's too dangerous, but I think of Ella. If George was seen in my father's study, it wouldn't be questioned—my appearance would be.

"I'll try, Master Lucas."

My heart pounds. "I need you to get it." I hope he can hear the pleading in my voice.

He bobs his head and leaves.

***

I'm a minute late to the meeting. I'm waiting for my father to call me out, but when he smiles at my arrival, my steps slow.

"Lucas," Aine sings warmly, and I take my seat beside Bernard and Cathal.

"We have two matters to discuss," my father starts.

The smugness on his face boils my blood.

"We need to vote in a new member."

"Have you anyone in mind, Master Andrew?" Brendan's words are measured, like he has heard rumors of who might be joining their elite circle.

"I do." My father glances at each of us. "Matthew Crowley."

I don't know him.

Aine smiles at me. "Isn't that Lucas's future wife's father, Master Andrew?"

"Yes. He will be a very fitting member. But I'm willing to hear everyone's suggestions." My father turns to me. "We shall start with you, Lucas. Who would you like to nominate?"

I don't care. "I personally think a female would be nice, since this circle is dominated by males."

I glance at Aine, and her agreement with me shines in her eyes. Anything that will hurt my father will drive me right now. He doesn't look pleased, and that makes me happy.

"Aine?" my father asks, but he already knows.

"I agree with Lucas, Master Andrew."

"Brendan?"

"Matthew Crowley has my vote."

My father smiles at Brendan, but that doesn't surprise me at all. Cathal holds the final vote, in theory, but my father will have the final say. He's also not stupid and understands the importance of keeping everyone happy. So my vote won't change things, but going against him will slow the process down a bit, as he tries to convince everyone that his way is the correct way.

"Cathal?"

Cathal glances at Aine before looking at my father. "I think I would like to hear who Aine and Lucas nominate before I make my decision." It's a small victory.

My father frowns. "We shall move on to our second matter." He shifts in his chair with irritation. "One of the ladies who was competing for my son's hand in marriage has broken one of the rules."

I hold my breath as I stare at my father. I sense the others glancing at me.

"Oh my!" I peek at Aine as her hand flutters to her chest.

"She was to marry Henry," Father continues.

Aine's mouth forms an *O*, her eyebrows rising into her hairline. No one asks questions; they all wait for him to painfully deliver what happened. My heart pounds and I hold still.

"She wasn't a virgin."

"Oh no." Aine's words have me wanting to take her hand off her chest and snap her fingers.

Hypocrites, all of them. Their sins stain far deeper than most people. I can't imagine Aine was a virgin when she got married, or any of them for that matter.

I hate the judgment being passed on Ella. So far, my father hadn't mentioned her name. But no doubt he would.

"Poor Henry." Aine's voice fills with pity.

I clench my jaw.

"He was devastated." My father lies so easily.

My heart pounds heavier in my chest as he exhales loudly, like the next sentence is taking a lot from him. "She must be punished."

"I don't think the chair should be used, Master Andrew," Aine says.

My chest aches as I picture Ella strapped to the chair.

"I do agree, Aine. It won't be. The rule once was that she should be hanged." My father lets that linger, waiting for objections, but no one says anything.

I glance at them all. They couldn't possibly pass that.

"But, I think we are beyond that as educated people." There's a lot of head nodding in agreement, but his words don't settle me. He has a glare in his eyes that makes me nervous. He's excited.

"Her crime is very serious, so I don't want to undermine our authority either. If we don't punish her, it will send out the wrong kind of message."

"What do you suggest we do, Master Andrew?" Brendan speaks up, and I want to leave the room. I want to go and get Ella and leave this place.

"I think she should be branded publicly. It will give us an opportunity to call the community together and also show everyone that it might be the twenty-first century, but we still follow rules."

I've never heard of the whole community being called together. My father wants to flex his powers, and with Ella, he can showcase how strong he is.

"I agree." Brendan speaks up.

"I agree." I am surprised at how quickly Cathal agrees, but to him, Ella is faceless. A rule breaker. Not a young girl who gave me her heart.

"What about the boy who took her virginity? What will happen to him?" I ask.

My father flashes me a warning.

"It is a fitting question, Master Andrew." Aine gives me her backing.

My father answers quickly. "My mother used to say to us, 'If there were no dirty women in the world, there would be no dirty men.'"

In other words, his word is final and only Ella will be punished.

***

My father keeps us there, talking about the upcoming branding, about rallying the people together. He delegates all the work over to the rest, and his eyes are alive.

I'm holding still. It's hard to bide my time, but once George gets me the key, I'm taking Ella away from here. I can't have her subjected to any more of this madness.

Once the meeting ends, I only grab what's necessary. My phone and my wallet. Everything else, we can buy as we need them. I have no idea where to go, but I can't stay here any longer.

I open the filing cabinet and place the box that holds Declan's finger into the drawer. It might help down the road. I lock the cabinet and pocket the key as the door opens.

George's brows knit together as he pulls at the cuff of his shirt before looking up at me.

"What's wrong?" I can sense his hesitation.

"The key isn't there."

"Maybe he moved it?" I would have to use something else to force the door open.

George still appears troubled. "Lucas, it was there. I saw it in the drawer earlier, when your father opened it while I was serving him tea."

"Maybe he moved it," I repeat.

"No. I don't think so."

I take a step toward George. "Say what you're thinking."

"I think someone else took it."

I move past George. There was no one else who would take it. Henry? But he doesn't like her. The moment I open the door, I'm aware of the darkness below me. My hand reaches for the switch, and I flick it up. No lights come on.

"I'll check the switchboard." George speaks directly behind me as I make my way down the steps. I don't know how many more I need to take before I reach the floor, but Ella's scream has me moving faster, and the steps disappear under my feet. I grip the banister as I land on the ground. I'm running toward her scream. Her cell door is wide open. Fear clutches me as her screams are cut off abruptly.

The lights flash on. Henry's hands are covering her mouth. Darkness blocks out everything as I rip him away from Ella.

His face pales as I spin him around. His mouth opens to speak, and I don't miss a beat as I slam him against the wall. My fist connects with his chin, sending his head flying back, and blood gushes as I smash my fist into his nose. He slumps, but I drag him back up and hit him repeatedly in the face.

"Lucas." George's voice rings in my ears.

I release Henry. His body hits the floor hard, but I can't look away. I want to pick him back up and keep going.

"Lucas, the car is ready."

I glance at George before reaching out to Ella. She flinches as I reach her, and I pause. I hate seeing the fear in her eyes. I hold out my hand and she glances at it, her eyes still wide with fear. Her small hand fits snuggly in mine, and I'm careful to be gentle when I close my fingers around hers.

"We're leaving." My words have her nodding, and she easily comes with me as I leave Henry bleeding on the floor. Once we're out, I close the door and lock it behind us.

George moves up the stairs to make sure we're clear. He waves us on, and we move to the garages. Ella trembles and I want to stop and assess her. After we get out of here, I promise myself that I can check every inch of her.

The car is running when we enter the garage. I open the door to let Ella climb in. She's numb as she ducks her head down, and I release her hand.

"Thank you, George." I'm not sure when we'll see him again. But I will always be grateful to him for helping us.

"Go, before he notices you're missing."

I don't linger any longer as I jump into the driver side. Ella stares at George, her hand plastered against the glass. I have no idea what's going through her head as I pull out of the garage. My stomach twists as we pass the fountain at the front of the house. I'm waiting to be stopped as I continue down to the main gates. When they open, I race out of them and toward freedom.

CHAPTER TWO

ELLA

The world moves past us so quickly. Trees shadow us briefly before sunlight cracks through the gaps and blinds me. As the sun sets, I can't let go of the image of George's face. Fear had twisted the old man's mouth. I blink and a tear falls.

"Sweetheart." Lucas's voice reaches me like the softest stroke, and I hunch my shoulders forward, not wanting to crack under the gentleness of his voice. I want to be left in this cocoon for now. My mind refuses to accept anything else, and right now, I want to be gentle with myself.

Fear shoots through me like a lightning bolt.

"Go back, go back." I grip Lucas's arm, and the car swerves.

"Ella, calm down." His words reach my ears, but they don't register.

"Go back, now."

Confusion pulls heavily at his brows.

I can't stop shaking my head. Why did I leave her behind? "We need to go back."

The car swerves to the left, and I nearly tumble into the door as Lucas stops the car abruptly.

I push myself back into a sitting position. "We need to get Hannah." My stomach twists painfully as my mind starts to paint detailed images of her torture.

Lucas shakes his head. "We are not going back." His words are softly spoken, but determination shines in his eyes.

"Yes, we are. We have to." I swallow bile.

"No." Lucas turns to start the ignition.

I grip his arm. "I'm begging you."

He looks away from me before glancing at me again. "No." His word has a finality to it that I refuse to accept.

"Lucas, he'll torture her." I say my fear out loud and allow it to twirl and form above my head until it almost feels real. Panic claws at me. I wrap my arms around my waist.

"We'll grab her and go, that's it. I promise." My breath is sharp, and when Lucas starts up the car, I swallow the saliva in my mouth. He's going back.

I try not to cry as a tremble enters my body. Lucas pulls back onto the road but doesn't turn around.

"What are you doing?" I glance out through the back window as Hannah grows further away from me.

"I'm not going back," he says through gritted teeth.

I'm staring at his side profile; his jaw is clenched, and I can't stop shaking my head.

"We can't leave her." Disbelief coats my tone.

"I can't risk you." His words come out in a growl.

I grip his arm again. "Why aren't you listening to me? It's Hannah." The sweet and innocent girl that will be hurt for being my friend.

"I don't care. We aren't going back."

I release Lucas's arm and stare at him. "I will never forgive you if you do this."

He glances at me now. "You will."

I want to scream in frustration. "Lucas, he will hurt her." I know I'm wrestling with someone who could easily flick me off.

"Let him. As long as he isn't hurting you, I don't care." The coldness in his voice has everything in me freezing.

"You're just like your father." The words leave my mouth, and his reaction is instant. His knuckles turn white as he grips the steering wheel.

My chest tightens as I struggle for air. "I'll go back the first chance I get."

Lucas glares at me. Black orbs pin me to the seat. Fear skitters along my spine, and my body can't take anymore. I break eye contact and close my eyes as I torment myself with images of Hannah.

Pain surrounds me as the car shifts under us. We don't speak, and night falls until the dark skies give way to small little lights that twinkle and sparkle. I used to think if I saw the first star, I could make a wish.

The word wish fell into the same category as fairy tale—nonexistent almost to the point of being cruel.

Lucas moves for the first time and turns on the heater. The angry part of me reaches out and knocks it off. I'm cold, but I intend to defy him at every turn until we can go back and get Hannah.

The hollow pit in my stomach has stretched with the distance we've put between ourselves.

I don't fall asleep, but I tumble in and out of awareness. It's like dipping your toe into hot water. I keep jerking upright from the faces that haunt me.

"We will be stopping soon." Lucas's voice sounds tight, and I refuse to look at him, but I'm grateful that we're stopping. My whole body is aching.

The lights of a motel flash up ahead. The car slows and Lucas indicates with the car's signal while driving into the deserted parking lot. The car grows silent under us; the only noise is the hum of the engine cooling down.

I don't look at Lucas but can sense his eyes on me. He gets out and my heart pounds as he walks around to the passenger side and opens my door. The cold air sends goose bumps rising along my body. The light summer dress and flip-flops are no barrier against the cold.

I climb out and tighten my arms around my waist. Lucas doesn't move, and I refuse to look up at him. I want to hug his torso. The thought has me digging my nails into my palms. The heat radiates from him, calling to me.

The door closes behind me. "Give me your hand, Ella."

I glare at Lucas. "No."

He steps in and I step back until I'm boxed in against the car. There's nothing friendly on his face as he dips his head so we're eye level.

"We need to go in here and not draw attention to ourselves. So, we're a happy couple looking for a room. Right now, you look like you're here against your will."

"That's because I am." My words are sharp, and I hope they cut him.

He doesn't ask for my hand again but pulls my folded arms apart and grips my hand. His hold is still gentle, and that pains me more. I want him to comfort me, but I also don't want his touch.

The clerk at the desk is listening to music. The white headphones are wireless and dangle from his ears. Lucas rings the small gold bell until it nearly falls off the counter.

Great job at not drawing attention to us. He looks like a big brooding bear.

The clerk pulls out the earphones and raises a brow.

"A twin room." Lucas speaks through gritted teeth. My hand still rests in Lucas's gentle hold, a complete contradiction to what I'm seeing.

The clerk glances away while running his tongue along his teeth. His mustard trousers are torn at the bottom, their length the cause of the shredded ends. They must have been dragging along the ground. His untidy appearance makes me wonder what kind of place this is.

"We only have a double bed."

My hand falls from Lucas, and he doesn't react. I'm not sharing a bed with him. My body immediately betrays me as a choir singing its chorus ignites in my blood.

"I'll take it." Lucas doesn't sound happy, and that douses some of the fire inside me.

Once he has the key, he pays cash and we walk along the doors, looking for our number. We stop at twenty-two, and Lucas unlocks the door. I don't want to go in. I don't want it to feel so final.

Lucas pauses but doesn't turn to me, and I know standing here in the dark and in the cold isn't going to make him go get Hannah. There isn't much warmth in the room. Lucas immediately starts fiddling with the dials on the one lone radiator that looks like it could use a good cleaning. I stand at the door and hug myself.

"It will heat up soon." Lucas pulls off his jumper, and I don't allow myself to take in the tight shirt that covers a chest I can almost paint with my eyes closed.

"Put it on. You're freezing."

I take the jumper and slide it over my head. I shiver as Lucas's body heat circles me, along with his smell. I lean my head in and sniff, taking comfort in his familiarity.

"Tomorrow, we will get you new clothes." He doesn't look at me as he moves around the room, opening drawers and presses. When he turns to the bed, it's the first time his eyes flicker to me, and I don't hold his gaze. I tighten my hold around my waist.

He marches to the bed and yanks off the gold duvet. It lands on the ground as he pulls back the duvet.

"It's clean!" he barks. His frustration grows as he continues to move around the room, closing curtains, checking the door. The light switches on in the bathroom as he pokes his head in.

"Use the bathroom and get some sleep." He sits on the bed with the remote in his hand. I hold my head high as I walk past him and into the bathroom. Once the door is closed, my chest tightens.

"She's okay," I whisper, but I don't believe the words for one second. I'm so angry for leaving her. She would have never left me.

I wash my face, and exhaustion has black circles forming under my eyes. I use the toilet before leaving the bathroom. Lucas still sits on the bed, the light from the TV flickering across his face. He looks tired, and I remember how he just left his whole world behind him to protect me.

"Get into bed, Ella." The coldness in his voice has my pity fleeing.

I fold my arms across my chest.

"Where are you sleeping?"

He glances up at me. "The bed is yours."

But that doesn't answer my question. He can't sleep on the floor, but I'm not inviting him into the bed either. I climb in and pull the duvet up over me. My body trembles with a new kind of exhaustion. Pain runs up and down my legs and sleep tugs at me, but each time I doze off, my body kicks out and I'm awake. Each time I wake up, Lucas is still sitting at the end of the bed. The TV is no longer on, but a light from outside shines through the thin curtains.

I move and try to find a better sleeping position. The bed shifts as Lucas gets up, and I move the duvet so I can see what he's doing. He's standing at the window, his wide back facing me as he stares out through a crack he created in the curtains. I bury my nose into his jumper and allow his scent to invade my senses. He is safety. He is love. I remind myself of that, and my body starts to relax.

But my mind won't settle. The keys of the car are sitting on top of the TV. My flip-flops are at the side of the bed. Once he's asleep, I'm going back for Hannah. I just need him to sleep.

"You can't stay there all night. Get into bed," I say, but he doesn't even move as my heart pounds.

"Go to sleep, Ella."

"I can't while you're lurking around the room," I snap and he turns to me. I grab a pillow and place it as a barrier between us.

"Just stay on your own side." I don't want to be too nice. I don't want him to see through my moment of kindness. Guilt tightens my stomach as his shoulders relax, and he steps away from the window.

I can't hold his eye as he kicks off his shoes and starts to pull off his shirt.

Now I'm wondering how wise it is having him beside me. I close my eyes and will my heart to slow down. The bed dips and the duvet shifts. I turn my back on him as my heart beats like a trapped rabbit.

Once he's asleep, I'll get the keys and sneak out. I have to get Hannah, and when I return, Lucas might be mad but he'll get over it. That's what I tell myself as I wait for him to sleep.

CHAPTER THREE

LUCAS

She's not asleep. Her breathing is too heavy. I want to remove the flimsy pillow that divides us. I roll onto my back as I stare up at the stained ceiling.

I'm not a saint, not even close. Lying here beside Ella and not touching her is a new kind of torture for me. It should be the last thing on my mind, with the situation we're in, but since I jumped into the car and took her from the house, all I've wanted to do is hold her and take what's mine. Take what I gave it all up for.

I glance over at her. She's holding still, but her whole frame is tense. She's not settled at all. She's going to try to get Hannah. I could see the determination in her eyes. She has no idea what she'll be walking back into, and I can't let that happen. This time, it won't be a public humiliation. It'll be worse.

I glance at the keys sitting on top of the TV. She checked them so many times that even if I had thought everything was okay, she would have made me suspicious.

I fight a grin. She really has no idea how easily I can read her. I removed the car key off the bunch. She really doesn't get that she's not leaving.

Not now. Not ever.

I turn back onto my side and face Ella's back. My jumper is still on her. She needs warm clothes; she needs food. I'm not sure if I can take her with me. Her fear for Hannah is making her unreasonable. I don't want to see Hannah hurt, but if that's the cost to keep Ella safe, I'm willing to pay it.

Her breathing sounds more level, and I wonder if the exhaustion has finally put her to sleep. My own body relaxes, and I want to remove the pillow between us. But for Ella, I don't. The erection pressing against my trousers isn't helping, but somehow I manage to fall into a light sleep. I'm not sure how much time passes when I feel the bed dip.

Blood pumps quickly throughout my body when I hear the careful jingle of the keys. She would never make a good burglar. The turn of the lock may as well be a gunshot in my ear as I open my eyes. I could stop this now, but the part of me that's angry wants to see how far she'll go. Will she stop and think of how stupid she's being? Will she worry about me waking up to find her missing? She's leaving me with no transport. I wonder if any of these things go through her mind.

The door closes, and I growl as I get out of the bed. I don't bother with my shirt or shoes. I won't be gone long. I part the curtains as she races across the parking lot. Her hair fans out around her as she runs in flip-flops. How easily she could fall and hurt herself. How silly she is sometimes.

But that's Ella—she throws herself into the face of danger, not caring what happens to her. I release the curtains and open the door softly. She's reached the car by the time I pull the door behind me, but I don't close it. Her head is bent as she goes through the keys. I hear her low curse when she realizes the car key isn't on the key ring. She's looking around her, scanning the ground. She hasn't even noticed me yet. I could be a robber or a rapist, and she's unaware of me. She's too busy bent down scouring the ground, and when she stands up, there's a rock in her hand.

What the hell is she going to do with a rock? "What are you doing?"

She screams, and her eyes snap up to me and widen. She's staring at my bare chest for a moment before she focuses on my face again. Her chest is rising and falling fast, and she holds the rock higher.

"Put the rock down now," I warn her as I move around the car. I'm too tired for this crap.

"I'll throw it."

Her threat has me pausing. "At me?" I grind out. She's testing me.

"At the car window. If you don't give me the key." She has the other hand held out like I might even consider her ultimatum for one second.

"If you throw the rock, the alarm will go off in the car." I inform her how stupid her choice would be.

"Yeah, and when people arrive, I'll tell them you took me."

There's a moment where I think she wouldn't, but I can see it, she would. I mentally give her points, but my irritation with her doesn't linger long on how brave she is.

I pretend to consider it for a moment.

"Here's the key." I take it out of my pocket and close the distance between us. She keeps the rock held high and I tut. "Drop the rock and I'll give you the key. I won't keep you here if you don't want to be here."

Guilt swirls in her eyes, and she exhales a wobbly breath, her eyes focusing on the key in my open palm. Her small hand reaches for the key carefully, like she's waiting for me to clamp my hand around hers.

I should. I should end this and not give her any false hope. But the angry part of me wants to see if she'll take it.

When she curls her fingers around it, she looks at me with a soft smile on her face.

"Thank you, Lucas."

The rock slips from her hand, and I feel no guilt as I pull her into my chest and spin her so her back is to me. I cut off her protest by covering her mouth with my hand. Wrapping my other hand around her waist, I lift her and carry her back to the room.

She jerks her body, and I feel the nip of her teeth along my hand. I don't pause but push the door open with my foot. Once we're in, I release her and slam the door behind us. She stumbles a few spaces away, and when she pushes her hair out of her face and looks up at me, her eyes are alive with outrage.

"You tricked me."

My own anger has me tightening my fists. "*You* tricked *me*. You waited until you thought I was asleep so you could sneak out of the room." I cut off the rest of my own words and shake my head. "Give me the key."

She still clutches it in her hands. She shakes her head while holding her chin high. "No."

I could force it from her, but I don't want to hurt her, and right now, too much violence is swirling around me. She was going to leave without a second glance. When she thanked me out in the parking lot and acted like I was going to hand her the key and let her drive herself right into danger, it made me understand that she has no idea what I would do for her, what I just did for her. What she is to me.

"Give me the key, Ella." My voice is a low growl, and I see her wavering for a moment.

as s "If I go now, I'll be back in a few hours."

I snap. I shouldn't, but the idea of Henry or my father getting their hands on her has me wanting the car key out of her hands now. She moves at the last second, launching herself to the left, and when I move to grab her, she screams and jumps up on the bed.

"She would never leave me, Lucas." She's holding out her hand as if it will stop me from getting up on the bed. Her words are meant to make me understand her reasoning for wanting to leave, but I can't see beyond the fact that she might end up getting hurt.

She screams again when I jump up onto the bed. Her eyes flicker to the right, giving away her next move, and when she jumps off the bed, I do too. She races for the door, but I get there first.

"We can keep this up all night. I quite like chasing you." I grin at her, and she swallows her uncertainty.

I'm angry and she can see it.

"Final time, give me the key."

I know she won't. I can see her taking two steps back, and I'm drained. So I end this.

I grab her, and it's easy to take it from her small hand. I pry her fingers open while trying not to hurt her. She bucks backward. Once I get the key, I have no idea what to do with her. The bathroom door is half-open. I move us toward it.

"Stop fighting me," I hiss in her ear as she tries to kick me. I open the door and push her in. I don't even give her a second before I pull the door closed and hold the handle.

It immediately starts to rattle in my hands, but I'm not letting her out. I take calming breaths as she thrashes against the door.

"How could you do this to me?" Her angry words penetrate the cardboard-thin door.

"How could you do this to me?" I fire the same question back.

"She's my friend, Lucas. They will hurt her."

I can hear the pain in her voice. She's right, they will hurt her, but I'm not going to confirm it. The only thing I need to do is calm her down.

"She'll be fine. No one will hurt her."

Silence falls and I'm wondering what she's doing. A bang against the door is followed by another bang.

"You're a liar."

I glance around the room. I can't stand here all night holding the door. Once she grows silent again, I move quickly, grabbing a chair and pushing it under the handle.

I listen, and she's moving around in the dark. I turn on the light for her.

"Are you going to let me out?"

I pick my shirt up off the floor and put it on. "Are you going to behave yourself?" I ask.

She doesn't answer me, and I take that as a no. Once my shirt is on, I slip into my shoes before hooking the car key back onto the key ring and putting them into my pocket. She would learn soon enough that I'm not letting her go. I'm protecting her, even if that means protecting her from herself.

CHAPTER FOUR

ELLA

I press my ear against the door, but I don't hear anything. Has he left the room? Doubtful. I feel so stupid. He hasn't even been asleep. I thought his breathing had sounded even. I felt like I had lain still for hours, until I feared I'd fall asleep. The timing had all seemed so right. I hated the idea of leaving him, but I reminded myself that I was going to be coming right back to him. I just needed to get Hannah out of there.

I lean my forehead against the door.

"Lucas?" He doesn't answer me. He really is pissed. He had left those keys there to see what I would do. I felt like a mouse caught in a trap.

He had tricked me.

"Lucas." Anger has me shouting his name.

"Be quiet." His voice is close but not right at the door.

I grip the handle and twist, but it doesn't budge.

I want to fight my way out of the room. I glance around the space, but there's nothing to use to pry the door open, and even if I get it open, then what? He's out there. I curse him. If he would only help me get her, this would all end. He can't really expect me to just forget about her.

I wonder if he has ever had a friend or anyone to fight for.

A small window above the toilet is questionable. I try not to make noise as I stand up on the toilet and push open the window. I pull myself up and look out. It's not high, but the window is small and it will be a tight squeeze. I glance back at the door, expecting to see Lucas standing there, but he isn't.

My heart pounds as I think about what I'm doing. I pause. I have no money, no way of getting back to her, but that small part in the back of my mind says I have to try. I could try to reason with Lucas. I'm staring out the window, my hands gripping either side as I think of ways to make him understand. The door opens, and if I thought he was mad before, now he looks murderous.

I hold up my hands as I turn to him. I want to tell him I wasn't actually going to climb out the window. He clears the floor in a few spaces, and I'm airborne as he throws me over his shoulder. Blood rushes to my head.

"Put me down now." He isn't giving me a second. I land with a thud on the bed as he stands over me and pins me to the bed with bottomless dark eyes.

"I think ..."

"Don't think." His words are growled at me. I can see he's struggling. His anger is always too much. I close my eyes and try to control my frantic heart.

"If you would let me explain." I open my eyes and regret it, as he bends over me with a look that scorches my skin.

"Explain why you were trying to climb out a window." He leans in closer, his fisted hands on either side of my head. "Explain why you were going to run off with no money, no car, nothing." He takes a deep breath. "You have no common sense."

His words sting. "I wasn't going to leave." I sound weak, but it's true. He doesn't believe me.

His eyes roam my face like he's trying to understand me.

"Lucas." I speak his name softly, and his eyes flicker up to mine. My heart rate spikes, and I try to ignore it. "If you could help me."

As he moves even closer, a vein bulges in the side of his neck. "I won't put you in harm's way. The end." His words are so final, and I hate him for them.

Tears burn my throat, and I want to wrap my arms around my waist, but he's too close to me.

"You have no idea what we're up against." His voice sounds like he's sneering at naïve little Ella.

"I think I do. I think I've been threatened enough by your *family* to know what I'm up against." I'm not being fair. I can see him flinch. I see the blame I've laid at his feet. But I'm not stupid. I get the danger.

"You're worried about Hannah." His tone has softened, and I wonder if I've finally gotten through to him. "And Jessie," he adds.

My stomach twists. I had fully intended to get her too.

"Maybe all the other girls too," he continues.

I see what he's doing.

"What about Alex? He was nice, and George, who helped us escape. What do you think will happen to him?"

I don't get to answer.

"What about your mother?"

Blood drains out of me, and my body turns to jelly. "My mother?" Saliva fills my mouth. "They would hurt my mother?" I'm shaking my head, begging him to tell me that isn't what he meant.

"Right now, everyone and everything you love is at risk."

Tears leak from the corners of my eyes.

"So who are you going to save? They won't stop until they have us." He pushes off the bed, his point really and truly driven home. I can't move. I feel if I do, I'll shatter.

My mother.

"We need to go back." It's the only way to end this. I sit up, and Lucas looks at me like I've lost my mind.

Brows draw down and dark angry eyes focus on me. "What?"

He heard me.

"You're now telling me everyone I love is in danger, so we need to go back now." My heart rate is rising along with my voice.

"No. We aren't going back." Lucas grinds out the word.

"We have to."

"There's no going back." His frustration has him turning away from me, but I can't accept that.

"You can't expect me to not go back when everyone I care for could be hurt or worse." My lip trembles as I try not to add the image of my mother to my chaotic mind.

Lucas spins and grips my arm. His hold is tight and painful. "You are all I care about. I need to keep you safe."

At the expense of me losing everyone else. I want to tell him that's not how this works, but I don't think I could get through to Lucas like that.

"You told me in the cell that you love me." My stomach flips when I think of his words. Even now, I can't stop the buzz that enters my system.

His eyes soften immediately, and his hold on me relaxes. He exhales heavily like he might be able to push all that anger away.

"I do love you." He leans in and my heart pounds at his closeness. When he lays his forehead against mine, I want to give up the fight and just let Lucas consume me. It would be so easy. It could be bliss with him.

"If you love me, you wouldn't do this to me." I say it and wait for the backlash, so I'm surprised when he laughs tenderly.

"I'm doing this because I love you." There's a smile on his lips.

I want to push him away. He isn't getting it. But his warmth, his smell, wraps around me like a warm blanket I want to snuggle under. He leans out slightly. I glance up and his eyes flicker to my lips.

"I don't want anyone to harm you again." He speaks with a smile as he pushes hair behind my ear. "You are all that matters to me now."

His words are offering so much, and when he leans in, his lips are so soft and warm that I want to melt in his arms. I want to give up and let him carry me.

"I can't just leave them."

His lips freeze against mine, and he steps away. It's only a foot, but it may as well be a mile. Instantly, I wrap my arms around my waist as he stares at me.

"My father has decided to brand you publicly for sleeping with me. It will be in front of thousands of people. You will become an example."

Horror skitters up my back. "Brand me?"

Lucas doesn't waver. "Yes, brand you. I couldn't let that happen. I had a window. It was small, but I took it and got you out. Now there will be a bounty on my head. I've broken the rules, Ella. My punishment will be severe."

I swallow as I think of Lucas being hurt. I'm trying to come up with some sort of plan, but getting back onto the property is dwindling away with the seconds that tick past.

"My mother?" He can't expect me to just leave her.

"George will let me know if anything happens."

I laugh, but it holds no humor. "So, what? We sit here and wait until they hurt someone? If we go back..."

He's shaking his head. "You don't get it. We can't go back. If we do, there's no forgiveness."

My legs grow weak, and I need to sit down. "They can't do that." I'm saying the words, but I know they aren't true. "We could go to the cops?" I offer up, and Lucas's eyes are looking more pained the longer I talk.

"They've been paid off."

I sit on the bed, no longer able to stand. "There has to be something we can do." I'm speaking to the floor, looking for answers from an old, thread-worn brown carpet. Lucas's feet come into view, and he hunkers down in front of me.

"I haven't given up, Ella." He pushes hair out of my face, and I immediately lean into his hand, seeking comfort.

"I need you to trust me. I'm doing everything I can to make this right."

I want to believe him. I want to lay all this worry on his shoulders. "How?" I know I sound like a broken record, but the fight in me won't die, not as long as there's breath in my lungs.

"There's only one thing I can do."

Something changes in the way Lucas looks at me now, and I can't fully decipher it.

"I need to remove my father."

"From the equation?" I ask, not sure what removing him means exactly. The world that Lucas lives in might be the elite of what our community is built on, but it's vicious and violent, two things I never expected to find.

"I'm not sure." He's being honest and that scares me.

I widen my eyes.

He smiles. Taking my face in his hands has my heart kicking up.

"I don't know yet. But I need you to behave. I can't spend all this time worrying about you leaving, when I need to focus on fixing this."

Guilt has me looking away. He must think I'm such a child, running off at every second.

"Ella."

When I peek back up, his eyes are lighter. "I love your bravery, but you need to trust me."

What he's asking for is huge. But I do trust him. I just have to believe that, for now, everyone will be okay. Even if it means lying to myself, I know I can't do anything to help them and neither can Lucas.

"I do trust you," I tell him.

He dips his head toward mine. "Thank you." His words break the last of my resilience, and I push my lips against his.

I have to believe we'll all be safe. It's a hard pill to swallow with no water.

CHAPTER FIVE

LUCAS

We're back in bed with only a few hours before the sunrise. Ella falls asleep almost immediately. I'm finding it harder. I'm not sure if she'll wake up and try to run again. I thought about tying her to the bed, but that would frighten her. She's placed the pillow between us, and I wait until she's fully asleep before I move it and tuck it behind my head.

I'm tempted to pull her frame into me, but my cock is rock hard, and having her closer would make this even harder. I tell myself to put the pillow back, but my head sinks deeper into it, forcing the pillow into place. Ella groans and turns on her side. She's facing me now, and the temptation is too much. I climb out of the bed carefully and let her sleep.

I glance back at Ella before slipping the phone out of my pocket. I only checked it a few hours ago, and I don't want to switch it on again. My father might have a tracker on it. I'm not how far he'd go. My disappearance won't go unnoticed with the upcoming branding of Ella and my wedding. No doubt the committee will start asking questions that he won't be able to answer.

I smile as I think of the shitstorm I've left him in. My smile fades as I glance back at Ella. She's exhausted and afraid, and I want to just keep her safe. She moans again, and I wonder what she's dreaming of. I return to the bed and slowly lie down, pulling the blankets over me. I can't face her, so I stare at the stained ceiling as she continues to move and groan every once in a while.

***

I wake to a warm stream of sunshine on my face and warmth beside me. My body is alert before my groggy mind can focus. I glance down at Ella, who's lying across my chest, her legs entwined with mine. My cock gets harder the more alert I become. Her face is buried in my chest, her breathing even. She's asleep. I stare at the stained ceiling and tell myself to do the right thing and detangle her from me. She needs her rest. She shifts her leg, inching closer to my shaft.

I turn and pull her into me, our bodies flush. Her head moves as she buries it into me again. I know the moment she feels me against her. She grows still and her heart starts to beat heavily against my chest. She's holding her breath. I keep my eyes closed as she tries to move out of my arms. I don't loosen my grip on her. I shift again, my erection pressing into her, and she freezes. When she starts to squirm again, I can't stop the groan.

"If you keep moving like that, I won't be able to control myself." She stops moving, and I open my eyes to find her wide-eyed staring up at me. The pulse flickers in her neck. She pulls her bottom lip in between her teeth.

"I need to go to the toilet," she confesses, and I have no choice but to let her go. She scampers from the bed and doesn't look back as she closes the bathroom door. After a minute, when she doesn't come out, I sit up in the bed.

"Ella." I force the warning into my voice. She better not be trying to escape. I get out of the bed and approach the bathroom door. It opens and Ella looks up at me, her cheeks flushed.

Her eyes flicker around the space, and she won't meet my eye. The pulse still pounds in her neck, and I think she might be nervous. Maybe I scared her this morning.

I step away from her and walk over to the window, where I sit down on one of the chairs. She climbs back into the bed, but she doesn't lie down. The quilts are held tightly in her hands, and I don't like how nervous she is. Her eyes are downcast, so I have no idea what's happening.

"I read your file," I say, and that gets her attention.

Wide green eyes stare up at me. "There's a file on me?"

She's so innocent to all that goes on around her. "Yes, your mother submitted all the information so we could learn about you before you arrived."

She seems so surprised. I'm waiting for her to ask me what it said, but she doesn't.

"I read a file on you too."

She read a load of lies I had made up.

"It says your favorite color is yellow, but I think that's untrue. I think it's black." Her cheeks are flushed as she speaks, and I can't help but smile at her.

"It is black." I wrote down nearly the opposite of the truth. At the time, I didn't think these girls had any right to know about me.

"It says yours is blue." I can't imagine Ella being untruthful like me.

"It is." She nods and the tenderness in her face has me shifting in my seat. How does she look so pure? I've never wanted to taint something so much.

"You have a fascination with typewriters," I say.

She smiles now. "I love the noise of them. It reminds me that someone is spinning a story that will change someone's life. And I also like the ding noise it makes."

I want to hear noises of pleasure dripping off those plump lips. I scratch my brow.

"You play chess?" she quizzes. "I don't see you having the patience for chess."

"I don't play chess, but I have the patience of a saint." I let my eyes trail across Ella. The fact I'm not buried in her is a testament to my patience.

"You've read the Bible?" It's another question, but her voice sounds shaky.

I smirk. "That one is true."

Her brows rise in surprise. "I didn't peg you as religious."

"I was trying to find a loophole for getting into heaven."

She laughs. "Did you find one?"

Her laughter has my trousers tightening with sinful thoughts. "No. But it kept my father happy."

He had drilled it into us, that there's someone more powerful than us and in order to be ready and strong, we needed to know what we were up against. So we had to read the man's story. The Bible. It was a painful and long experience. At times, some stories clung to me, but overall it went right over my head.

"You collect stones?" Out of all the girls, Ella's file caught my attention because I had thought it odd. Now, looking at Ella it fascinates me, and I'm like a child with all the why's.

"It started with my grandmother's grave." She shrugs. "I took a stone off her grave to have with me. It was like she was with me." Ella's brows draw together. "So when I went somewhere that I liked, I took a stone or pebble from it. I don't know. It just made me feel more connected."

She won't look at me, and once again, I'm tempted to climb onto the bed and tilt her head back so I can see her eyes.

Her eyelashes lift, giving me access. "It's funny, you know." She's twisting the blanket between her fingers. I'm not sure if she's even aware of what she's doing. "I didn't take one from my dad's grave. I was so young. I was afraid if he did stay with me, and I would see him…" She rolls her pained eyes like she's being silly. "Like you know…" She shrugs again.

She didn't want to see him after he hung himself. I can hear what she's saying, and the pain on her face has me tightening my fists.

I'm angry at a ghost for hurting her.

I want to change the subject, but I don't want her to think I'm not grateful for how much she's sharing with me.

"It's silly and now a part of me wants a stone from his grave." She's half smiling, but it's all twisted up in her pain.

"When all this is over, I would be honored to take you there."

Her nostrils flair and her hand flutters to her chest. She blinks and nods. "I think I'd like that very much."

She's smiling but still hurting.

"So what's our plan for today?" She seems more upbeat now, and I take it and sit up in the chair. I need to ring George. This feels like I'm flying blind, and I need to know exactly what's happening.

"I think you should shower." That thought alone has me shifting in the chair. "I'll go and get us clothes and food."

I stand and look out the window while trying to rearrange myself.

"You're going to go clothes shopping for me?"

I turn at Ella's amused voice. "Yes. A size six on top and eight on the bottom." I need to leave the room. My thoughts are too unpure.

Ella smiles sweetly up at me, and for one second, I question if she's deceiving me. It wouldn't be the first time.

She must see the change in me, because her smile dwindles away to nothing.

"Do I need to tie you up?" I ask, taking a step toward the bed.

"Tie me up?" Her brows rise.

"Are you going to behave while I'm gone, Ella?"

"Oh." She laughs, and now I wonder what she was thinking.

I grin. "I can tie you up for other reasons if you want."

Her face flames, and she holds her head high. "While you're gone, I'll shower and tidy the room."

"Remember, I have the car, the money, and if you run…" Now I'm considering bringing her with me. Am I taking too big of a risk?

She folds her arms across her small chest like I've offended her. "Are you going to keep this up the whole trip?"

I smirk. It's nice that she sees this as a trip and not an absolute upheaval of our lives. A rearrangement of what we know. A fucking mess.

"I won't be long," I settle on, and she unfolds her arm like she won. Yet I can't seem to leave the room. Fear of her running has me thinking of using the bedsheets to tie her to the bed.

"Okay," she says slowly, like she has to for me.

"I need my jumper." I don't really. I'm stalling.

She pulls my jumper off. The thin white straps of her summer dress show so much skin, and it's distracting. She throws the jumper and I pick it up. It smells just like her. I pull it on and know I can't stall any longer.

"I won't be long," I reinforce, and she nods like she's wondering why I'm still standing here.

I pull the door behind me as I step outside. I glance back in the window. I'd left a crack in the curtain and can see she's lying back in the bed, staring up at the ceiling.

I take out the phone and turn it on. I give a soft laugh as Ella stares at the ceiling. Her lips are moving, and she covers her face with both hands. She looks crazy. When she draws her hands away, her face is red, and she gets up abruptly. I turn away from the window and ring George.

He answers on the second ring. He knows we need to keep it brief. "All the girls have been sent home except for Hannah and Jessie. They're both being kept here, accused of assisting in Ella's escape."

I knew my father would pull some stunt like that. But he's really circling Ella out. I had thought he would cover this up a bit longer.

George clears his throat. "Sandra Crowley's father has put a bounty on your head."

I sneer. "How much?"

"Five million."

I want to ask dead or alive, but I don't.

"I'm going to forward you a number for someone who can help you, Lucas."

Is this a trap? I don't know, but my time is running out.

"Okay. Thank you, George." I hang up with just under three seconds left, which I always stick to.

I have to believe that George is on my side. He's all I have left. I glance back into the room but can't see Ella. The bathroom door is closed. If I'm going to go, I need to go now. I hastily make my way to the car. The quicker I go, the quicker I can get back, and Ella better be here.

CHAPTER SIX

ELLA

I glance out the window. He's in the car. He has a phone. It just keeps circling around in my head. He's in contact with someone. I could have rung Hannah and made sure she's okay. Why did he keep that hidden from me?

I could have rung my mother.

My heart pounds as he drives away. There's an urge to start running, but it's stupid and pointless. I wouldn't get far.

My mind won't settle. I need that phone! I start to make the bed we shared. Waking up in Lucas's arms had every nerve in my body on fire, and then I felt his excitement. He was perfect, with his tousled hair and dark eyes. My cheeks burn as I fix the duvet.

I wanted him so badly, but I was overthinking it and got too nervous. I hadn't even brushed my teeth, and I didn't want to breathe on him.

I tried to brush my teeth with my finger in the bathroom, but it was disgusting.

I finish the bed and enter the bathroom. I avoid the mirror, knowing how bad I look. No wonder he sat on the chair by the window.

I had thought he was dropping little sexual hints throughout our conversation, but it was my dirty mind. When he mentioned tying me up, all kinds of thoughts raced through my head. My chest burns now with mortification. He had been worried about me running off.

I strip and get into the shower. The water is lukewarm, and I wash quickly with the smallest bar of soap in existence. The shampoo bottle is tiny—the length of my baby finger. I use it all and then feel guilty leaving none for Lucas.

The thought of Lucas in the shower has my mind skipping back to the day we shared a shower together.

His damaged hands, which still hadn't fully healed, has me frowning. I wash quickly and get out. The towel is tiny, and no matter which way I put it, it still only covers my important bits. I use the hand towel to dab-dry my hair.

Rubbing the steam off the mirror, I stop drying my hair. I look different. I look older. The glass slowly steams back up, and I gather my clothes off the floor. I'm not putting them back on. I'll wait until Lucas returns with fresh clothes. I keep the bra out. I'll get to wear that again, as I can't imagine Lucas bra shopping.

I check the wardrobe for a dressing gown, but there isn't one. There's only a pair of off-white slippers that look worn. I'm not putting my feet in them.

I climb up on the bed with the remote and turn on the TV. It's weird to have control over what I'm watching. With my mother, she made sure it was appropriate for me to watch. Basically, it was all PG and educational. At the house, we got to watch crime shows or movies that were also created with children in mind.

As I flick from one talk show to another, I decide that I haven't really been missing much. A stage is set up with four people sitting on chairs. One is accusing the other of sleeping with his brother, who smiles smugly. The presenter is waiting for DNA results for her first child to see which brother is the father. I watched the drama unfold for over an hour. It ends up neither of them are, and I giggle at the stupidity of it all. They're acting. There's no way that it's real.

The door opens and Lucas steps in with bags in both hands. When his eyes clash with mine, it's like he freezes, and I remember the tiny towel that's barely covering my vital bits. He kicks the door closed with his foot without looking away from me.

I get that feeling that I often get with Lucas, like stepping into a lion's cage. I scamper off the bed while turning off the TV.

"I didn't want to get into my dirty clothes."

It takes him a moment, but he moves and places the bags on a table positioned at the window.

"I have stuff here for you." He works with his back to me, moving stuff from one bag to the other. When he's done, he turns to me. His dark eyes swim and my body hums. He holds one of the brown bags and walks to me with it. Each step has my heart pounding a bit faster.

"Thank you." I take it and peek in and am surprised to see so much black.

"You're welcome." His voice is deep, and I slowly look up at him. I still haven't brushed my teeth, but he's so tempting, like a low hanging fruit that's begging to be plucked.

I step closer until my chest brushes his. My heart starts to dance as I reach up on the tip of my toes and plant a kiss on his lips. It's a flick of a switch. I'm airborne as he picks me up, and I'm cushioned by the bed. He hovers over me and I swallow. He doesn't miss a beat as his lips slam down on mine, consuming me.

His hands are hungry as they roam across the towel. My breasts immediately react to his touch, my nipples brushing the towel, and I groan into his mouth. I want to remove the towel and let him wriggle closer. I can feel his erection, and it terrifies and excites me.

His breathing is labored and swirls with mine. "I want this so badly. I really do.Bbut I need to feed you first." He talks into the pillow like a dying man, and I'm not sure if I should laugh or object.

My stomach growls, and he pushes himself off me reluctantly. When he looks up at me, I can see his restraint wavering. I feel powerful with how he's watching me.

"Go get dressed." It sounds like a growl.

I scoot off the bed and pick the bag up off the floor. When I enter the bathroom, he hasn't moved. I close the door and drop the towel, and I don't want to test his control. A cold shower is looking very appealing now.

My stomach rumbles again, and I pull on the clothes. The black bra and underwear are a surprise. They're lacy and fit perfectly. My black trousers are snug, and I add a black jumper that rises each time I brush my hair out. The clothes are tight and fit me like a glove.

I take out the toothbrush and toothpaste that's also in the bag, along with deodorant. He had thought of everything. It feels like heaven when I finally get to brush my teeth.

The only color is the bright pink socks. The sneakers are also black, and I slip my feet into them. I feel strange in these clothes, as I'm so used to dresses and gowns. I feel self-conscious when I step out into the room. Lucas has his back to me, and he's swapped his shirt and jumper for a black T-shirt that stretches across his back. The trousers are the same from yesterday. My stomach twists. He's setting the small table.

"Smells lovely." I'm nervous, which is silly. He glances at me and returns to what he's doing before he fully turns back to me.

His eyes start at the top of my head and move all the way down to my feet.

"You really like black," I say as he continues to drink me in.

"It's my new favorite color." He takes a step toward me.

"I thought it was already your favorite color."

He reaches me and exhales loudly. "It's my new favorite color on you."

Taking my face in his hands, he kisses me. It's soft and I can feel the effort he's using to hold back.

He releases me and steps back to the table. "Now we eat."

I sit down to our first meal together. French fries and a burger. I even get a coke.

I start with a French fry. I'm aware he's watching me. I glance up at Lucas, and I can't stop the smile. "I can't eat with you watching me."

His smile is wide. "Your mouth is fascinating and very distracting."

I pick up a fry and place it into my mouth. Covering my mouth with my hand, I chew.

"Is that better?" I ask.

His eyes are so light, and I want to take him to a mirror and let him see what I see.

I lower my hand and try not to smile too much as I chew, but it's hard when he's looking at me like that.

It's on the tip of my tongue to tell him that I love him. I let my lids close as I focus on opening my coke. When this is all over, I will.

We eat between bites of heaven and secret smiles. It's bliss. It's what fairy tales should be made with: burgers, motels, and pink socks. Yeah, this is my fairy tale. My heart swells, and I laugh.

"What?" Lucas has nearly all his food gone, but he hasn't looked away from me the whole time.

"I'm happy," I say after a moment.

His eyes grow even lighter. "I got you something." He stands up and takes something small out of his pocket. He looks at me again before sliding his hand across the table. "It's small, and I just thought…" He's being awkward, and it's cute.

"Just give me my present." I pry his large hand off the table, and my heart beats a bit faster. It's a key ring.

I pick up the mini typewriter key ring. "Thank you." My first present.

"It's nothing. I just saw it on the rack and grabbed it."

I'm smiling again at how awkward he is. "I love it."

He relaxes and smiles. I don't finish all the food. My stomach can't take handle more bite.

I hold up my key ring to the window so I can see the details. It's very well done, and the fact he got this for me has me glancing at him. He isn't watching me but stares out the window. He's frowning, and I lower my key ring.

"What's wrong?"

He sits up and shakes his head. "I think we have somewhere to go. I'm just waiting on an update."

This is the perfect opportunity to bring up the phone. "Like a phone call?" I ask as innocently as I can.

He sits straighter, his eyes darkening. "Yes."

It's a quick answer.

"Maybe I could make a phone call."

"No."

I hate it when he does that. Yes, no. One-word answers with no explanation.

"It would really put my mind at ease."

"It's too dangerous." He stands and starts tidying up the food.

"One phone call, Lucas. Please?"

His hand curls around the brown food bag. His eyes snap to mine. "I'm sorry, Ella. But you can't."

He isn't sorry at all. "I can't go and see if Hannah's okay. I have to stay here and just keep imagining what my friend is suffering because of me." "Now I can ring her, and it's a no too?"

"Are we going back there again?" Lucas's voice is cold and calm. I want to poke him.

"Yes, and we will keep revisiting because I won't forget about her."

He grips the bridge of his nose. "The phone might be tracked. It's too risky." He holds up his hands. "Even if it wasn't, how would you ring Hannah? Do you have a number for her?"

I don't and ringing his house is stupid. "I could ring my mother." I know *her* number.

Lucas's eyes soften, but he isn't giving in. "No. I'm sorry."

I turn my back on him while gripping my key ring. "Okay. I'm sorry." I exhale loudly before turning around. "It would just be nice to hear her voice, but I understand."

His eyes are filled with suspicion. "When it's safe, I promise I'll let you ring her."

I nod. I saw him on the phone. He spoke to someone, so this isn't fair. I can see he won't bend. So I nod again.

He relaxes. "Okay, I'm going for a shower." He finishes tidying up the table and grabs another brown bag that must hold his new clothes. He pauses at the bathroom door.

He wants to say something, maybe issue a final warning, but when I sit down on the bed and pick up the remote, he seems more content going into the bathroom. I stare at the closed door and listen for the running water.

I just need to get the phone. If I could just hear my mother's voice, I would hang up. That's it. I would have it back in a minute. All I had to do was creep in and take it out of his pocket without him noticing. Yeah, easy peasy.

CHAPTER SEVEN

LUCAS

The shower is pitiful, but I need it. My body is tense with wanting Ella. My shaft is sore, and I need to relieve myself, but I can't. I'm too wound up. I felt like a monster when she asked to make a phone call. It's too risky, and I'm not risking her. I scrub my hair and body and rinse off.

I pause, thinking I heard a noise. Rinsing off the suds, I pull the shower curtain back. The bathroom is empty. I'm being paranoid, but with a five-million-dollar bounty on my head, I have no doubt we're being followed, and any wrong move will get us caught. I get out of the shower and dry off.

I still haven't got an update from George on our new location, and that's making me nervous. He's taking too long. I feel like a sitting duck here.

I finish cleaning and get redressed. Pulling up my jeans, something feels off; the weight isn't right. My stomach plummets. The noise I heard. She wouldn't...

I search my empty pockets.

I'm out the door, and my heart gallops as I look around the empty room. She left. My brain is on a loop until I spot the car keys still on the table.

I open the door, and she turns around, her face white as she clutches the phone.

I take the phone out of her hand, and she doesn't struggle. Bringing it to my ear, I listen.

"Ella." It's an older female voice. I assume it's her mother. Staring at the screen, I see one minute on the timer as I close it.

I can't speak; I'm that angry. I turn and enter the motel room. I hear the click of the door as she follows me in and closes it.

I can't look at her. My heart beats too fast, and I need to calm down.

She's wise enough not to speak. How long would it take them to trace us? One or two minutes? I kept all calls no longer than a minute. The phone feels like a timer in my hand when it rings.

I glare at Ella, and the remaining color drains from her face. I open the phone and listen.

"Ella." It's her mother. The number is blocked, so she isn't alone. Someone was counting on Ella ringing her, and now they have our location.

"We need to leave now." I start grabbing our few belongings. I pack up the bathroom and get my shoes on.

"Why? She won't tell anyone."

I can't even look at Ella. I glance around the room. We have everything. Taking the two bags, I march to the car, and Ella follows.

"Lucas, why are we running?"

"Get into the car," I bark and dare her to defy me.

She climbs in while huffing. I don't let her buckle up before I pull out of the parking lot.

I can't stop staring at the rearview mirror. A black vehicle stays close to us. I take a left, and it takes a left too.

"Put on your seat belt," I tell Ella.

"Not until you tell me what's going on. My mother won't tell anyone."

I grip the steering wheel and check behind us again. "We're being followed," I bite out, not really wanting to explain anything to her right now. I'm so angry.

The click of her seat belt eases me slightly. I take a right, and the black vehicle doesn't follow. I'm being paranoid. I take a breath for the first time since we left the motel.

"They must have been with your mother waiting for you to ring." I speak my thoughts out loud. She must have been told that I took her daughter. God only knows the lies my father spun.

"People are with my mother? What if they hurt her?"

I glare at Ella. "They want to hurt you."

She flinches as I shout at her. I grip the steering wheel and try to calm down. A navy vehicle moves behind us.

"I'm trying to keep you safe." My calmness isn't coming, and the more I think of what she did, the more anger strangles me.

"I can't trust you," I finish as I glance in the mirror to see the vehicle still behind us. I take a right off the freeway, and it follows. I drive within the speed limit, and the vehicle cruises behind me. I can't see the driver with the line of tint that covers the top of the window screen.

I glance at Ella. She hasn't spoken. She's staring out the window, her shoulders shaking.

"Are you crying?" My words come out in a growl.

She won't answer me. "Ella," I warn.

She shrugs. "Leave me alone." There are tears in her voice.

Guilt twists my stomach into knots. I glance in the rearview mirror as I slip back onto the freeway. I'm expecting the vehicle to veer off just like the black one, but this vehicle follows. I sit up a bit straighter.

We are being followed. I glance at Ella, and she's still staring out the window.

"Stop crying." My voice is a fraction away from a growl, and I don't mean to sound so angry. I really want her to stop crying. I hate it.

"I'm not like you. I can't just switch it off." Her words sting, and I know she has no idea of how deeply they cut.

"I just needed to hear her voice." She continues to cry as she speaks.

I glance in the mirror again, and the vehicle is still following us. I push my foot down heavier on the gas.

"She's my mother. I was afraid she wouldn't answer." She tries to make me understand. The vehicle behind us matches my speed.

Fuck.

"She's all I have left. You must understand that. I love her, and the thought of someone hurting her is just torture." She's facing me now.

I take a quick peek at her. "Okay," I say as I refocus on the road.

"Okay?" she questions.

I don't want to panic her. "We're being followed."

"I know. You said that like ten minutes ago."

"I was wrong then."

She turns around in the seat.

"Ella, don't turn around."

She sits forward. "Everything I do is wrong."

She is beyond emotional right now. Hearing her mother's voice really took over everything.

"We lost them," I lie to allow her to wallow. I keep driving and slip on and off the freeway. The navy vehicle stays close to me. He has to know that I'm aware that he's tailing me. For five million dollars, he won't let me out of his line of sight for a second.

"You think people are in our home hurting her?"

"I don't know," I answer.

"What?" She sounds devastated.

"I can't focus right now, Ella."

She sits up. "We are still being followed, aren't we?"

"Yes."

"You said we lost them." The accusation in her voice has me glancing at her. I want to point out that this is because she wouldn't listen to me, but tear marks are still visible on her cheeks.

"We didn't. It's Sandra."

"Sandra's following us?" Disgust coats Ella's words, and a knot in my stomach unravels as I force down a smile.

"Sandra's father put a bounty on me. Five million dollars." I glance at Ella.

Her mouth hangs open, and she closes it. "Five million dollars?" She's shaking her head.

I leave the freeway and drive until we hit the next city. It's busy, but the traffic flows steadily. The navy vehicle has tucked itself right behind me.

"Yeah. I think it's safe to say she's a daddy's girl," I say as I pull into a parking lot.

"When they get you, what happens?" Ella's voice is small.

"I don't know, but we're very close to finding out."

I drive close to a wall that we could jump across. I see a crowd of people on the other side and a shopping mall beyond that. We need to get there and lose our tail in the masses.

"I'm going to stop the car now, and when I get out, we're going to run. Don't stop, just run."

"What?" Ella sounds terrified.

I don't blame her. "Ella, I need you to say yes, that you understand."

She nods, and I pull up the handbrake, stopping the car abruptly, and jump out. When I reach Ella's side, she's out, and I grip her hand and start to run.

The navy vehicle stops, and two men jump out. My eyes clash with the driver's, and he's moving fast toward us. We reach the wall, and I help Ella up. I grip the wall and pull myself over it. Landing on the other side, I grab Ella's hand, and we jog into the crowd. It takes so much for me to stop running. But running through a walking crowd would attract too much attention.

I glance over my shoulder and quickly face forward. They were close to us. I move quickly but still keep it at a walk. The mall is up ahead, and it's there that I hope we get lost in the crowd.

CHAPTER EIGHT

ELLA

Lucas's grip on my fingers is crushing, but I don't say anything. I had just wanted to hear my mother's voice and to make sure she was okay. She asked me where I was and who I was with, but I didn't answer her questions. I just needed her to tell me that she wasn't being tortured or hurt. Relief at hearing she was okay was short-lived when Lucas stood at the motel door. The look in his eyes was murderous.

We enter the mall. I've seen them on TV, but I've never been in one. The child in me is taking it all in. Shop windows filled with products of every kind move past us quickly. Lucas pulls me closer as he glances over his shoulder.

He looks up. "We'll slip in down here."

I follow his gaze to a toilet sign. People glance at us as we move past them, and I'm not sure if we look odd to them or if it's that we're walking so fast. Lucas must notice too, as we slow down. My feet match his, but my heart still races with fear.

The phone in his pocket bleeps, and without slowing down, he takes it out and runs his fingers across the screen.

I notice how every female we pass gives Lucas a second look, their eyes appreciative as they travel over his physique. I tighten my hold on his hand, and he peeks down at me before slipping the phone back into his pocket.

"It's okay," he tries to reassure me as we veer down the tunnel. Lucas glances over his shoulder again, and his hand tightens even further.

We obviously haven't lost them. Double doors at the end of the tunnel draw closer.

"When we get out these doors, run." He speaks while his feet move faster. I have to half run just to keep up with him.

"Ella, you have to answer me."

I swallow. "Yes, I'll run."

Lucas slams down on the bar and an alarm rings. For a moment, I'm frozen, until Lucas tugs me and air moves past my face. We run down an alley, sidestepping bins and palettes from recent store deliveries.

We enter a courtyard that's empty.

"Stop." My heart pounds at the deep voice. Lucas spins us around, and everything drains from my body. The man is facing us, holding a gun.

Everything disappears as Lucas pulls me behind him, hiding me from the gunman. But what about him? I'm no longer holding his hand. My hands instinctively touch his back.

The air won't fill my lungs quick enough, and my throat squeezes with terror.

The man has a gun.

"If you just come with me, this ends," the man says, and my body hunches closer to Lucas's.

"I'll double what they're paying you." Lucas's voice rumbles through the hand I have pressed against his back for comfort. I need to tell myself that he's still standing here. That we will be fine.

I should have never touched the phone. My brain is telling me to bolt for the large green gate to my left. My fingers instinctively dig deeper into Lucas's T-shirt. I want to close my eyes and curl into a ball.

"He said you would say that." The man sounds like he's smiling.

The screech of a door has Lucas spinning, and we're running again. He grips my arm, and he's half dragging me as we slip through a side gate. Lucas knocks bins over as we run.

"Hey!" I glance over my shoulder at the angry security man who shouts after us, but Lucas doesn't slow. I stumble over my feet and nearly fall. Lucas keeps me upright before he ducks into a cab. The door slams. He's telling the driver to go.

We're moving, and I glance out the back window. The man stops running, but his eyes bore into me. Lucas pulls me away from the window, and into him. His hold is too tight—it's suffocating, and when I push away, he loosens his grip.

"Where to?" The cab driver speaks, but I keep my eyes closed as I allow the feel of Lucas to calm my pounding heart.

"Train station." Lucas sounds breathless, and my hand flutters to his heart, which is pounding harshly under me.

"It's okay. We're safe," I tell him, without looking up into his eyes. I'm sure he's still angry with me, and right now, I don't blame him. I just want him to relax. Having him hold me is like being held by a brick wall. A kiss burns my forehead, and I test a quick peek. Our eyes meet, and any bravery I felt skittered away. I shrivel under his gaze. It's crushing and lethal, and I can't hold his eyes.

The back of the driver's seat becomes my focus as I will my heart to slow. I don't move my hand from Lucas's pounding heart.

"He had a..." The brick wall tightens around me. I can't say the word *gun*. This is serious. Would they have shot us if no one was around?

A shiver assaults my body.

The cab slows, and Lucas finally lets me go. I take in a lungful of air as he pays the cab driver. Lucas opens the door and captures my hand in his again as we start walking through the crowds of people. Today is so many firsts for me, but I can't take it all in. I'm going to be on an actual train. The little bit of excitement is extinguished as Lucas pulls me closer. I don't dare look at him again. I stay quiet beside him as he pays for two tickets.

We enter the train, and Lucas moves us through several cars before we stop at our seat numbers. A large plastic white table sits in the middle. We move around it. Lucas makes me go in first so I'm at the window, and he sandwiches me. Our thighs are tight together, and I want to tell him to give me some space.

Lucas stares out at the walkway as people enter, and when the train starts to move, it's the first time he relaxes. He releases my squashed hand.

I flex my fingers and watch the crowds of people mesh together until they become one long strip of color before they melt into gray, and I stop staring out the window as we move through a tunnel.

I have so many questions. Like where are we going? Was that man really going to shoot us? Is my mother okay? How much trouble are we in? Is Lucas okay?

"Tickets." My heart ping-pongs around my chest as the ticket man approaches us. I need to breathe before I give myself a heart attack. Without a word, Lucas hands over our tickets. The man punches them before moving on. I lick my dry lips and chance a quick peek at Lucas. He's staring down the aisle, but from his side profile, I can see a muscle working in his jaw.

I had been so stupid. I want to apologize, but it dies on my lips when Lucas turns to me. His eyes have a savage look in them that has me shifting closer to the glass.

"It's okay." His words are meant to reassure me, I think, but they're barely intelligible.

He releases me from his hold and runs his hands across his face. Tears burn my throat. I really messed up.

My hand shakes as I touch his back. He stiffens under my touch. "I'm sorry," I whisper, and when he looks at me, the savagery turns into confusion before it all melts away, and I'm looking at Lucas.

He's shaking his head. "It's not your fault."

My vision blurs. It is. I know that now. I need to start listening. I could have gotten both of us killed.

"I'm really sorry."

He reaches for my face, and his thumb captures a fallen tear. "I'm not mad at you, Ella. You think I'm mad at you?"

I'm nodding at his question. Mad is an understatement. My chest tightens as he tilts his head.

"I'm mad I put you in this situation." He leans his forehead against mine, and his breath fans across my face. He grips my face with his hands, and I do the same to him.

"He had a gun." I say my shock out loud.

Lucas's hands tighten on my face. "Shh. It's okay."

I'm not sure if he's trying to soothe me or him. But I allow myself to relax in his hold. He releases my face, and I slowly take my hands off his. I don't want to let go, but I'm happy when he tucks me into his side. I wrap my arms around his waist and listen to his heartbeat as it slows and finds a steady rhythm. The train moves under us, and I allow my body to fully relax.

When I wake up, I'm still in the same position. Raising my head off Lucas's chest, I stare up into his handsome face. He's asleep. His inky lashes are resting on his cheeks. With his eyes closed, he looks angelic. A small smile tugs at my lips. I want to trace his face with my fingers.

"Remember," I whisper. It was something I saw on TV. We lose so many memories and moments through time. If you tell yourself out loud to remember, your brain will store it away in a place that's at the forefront of your mind. I'm not sure how much truth is in that, but I'm willing to test the theory.

I don't think my mind could forget Lucas anyway, but I want to remember him, right now, as the light flickers across his face. He's silent; no war rages in his eyes. He's still and almost at peace.

"You know it's bad manners to stare." His lips move, and heat scorches my cheeks, but I don't move away. His lids flicker up, and his eyes focus on my face before they flicker to my mouth.

I smile. "I thought you were asleep," I defend.

He clears his throat and sits up straighter. "I was." He wrestles with a smile.

"I'm sorry for everything." I've apologized already, but I know how much I messed up this time.

"How sorry?" Lucas looks so serious, and my heart pounds.

"I wish I could turn back time," I say, knowing that if I had this knowledge, I would never have touched that phone.

"I will forgive you under one condition."

His serious tone has me swallowing, and it's like the old Lucas, the one who got his kicks off by punishing people.

The smile he was wrestling with earlier wins, and my heart gallops. "A kiss."

I frown and pull away. I want to scold him for scaring me.

His smile vanishes. "I want you to kiss me."

The way he says it makes me feel nervous. Like he'll judge my heart through my kiss. I wronged him, so I hold my head high and move closer to him. He doesn't make it easy, and he doesn't pull me in or close his eyes. He sits back and doesn't take his eyes off me.

I touch his chest, and I feel the beat of his heart. As I lean in, he keeps his eyes trained on me, even as my lips touch his. I can't close my eyes. I can't cut him off like that. I press my lips heavier against his, and he doesn't respond. My heart races. I'm not sure what to do. Give him more? I lean out slightly and run my finger along his lips.

His eyes are soaking everything up; all the light around us gets pulled into the vortex of Lucas, and I can't take much more. I close my eyes and kiss him deeply. His lips don't move under mine, and I pull his bottom lip in between my teeth and nip it. He twitches under me, and I smile into the kiss. Flicking out my tongue, I lick his lip where I bit it, and he groans. I stop the kiss as my body starts to react, and I remind myself we're on a train with other passengers.

He's breathing heavily under me, and I lean back in my seat, feeling powerful. I glance at him and smile at my victory. "Am I forgiven?"

He tilts his head as he exhales a heavy breath. "Yes."

His one word is so serious, and I can't stop the laugh that bubbles up into my throat.

Lucas pulls me into his side and plants a kiss on the crown of my head. I bask in his love. The thought of losing him causes an actual pain in my chest.

"This is really serious," I say while running my hand across the white plastic table.

"Thirty years ago, my father had an affair with a member of the community. She got pregnant, and Henry was born."

I sit up and stare at Lucas. "I'm so sorry." Henry is his half brother. How is his father still in power after such an act? I don't ask questions.

Lucas waves off my apology. "I'm telling you this so you can really see what's happening. No more secrets."

I'm nodding like an eager dog.

"No more doing things behind my back, Ella." His warning has embarrassment burning my face.

"I know." My voice sounds harsh, but I don't want to be reprimanded like some child. I know I messed up.

A ghost of a smile touches his lips but disappears as quickly as it appeared. "My mother found out about the affair and ended up hurting Sorcha."

My heart stills in my chest.

"She killed her, and my father covered it up."

I swallow the saliva that pools in my mouth. "You're talking about murder?" I don't think I want to know what's really going on. This couldn't be real—men with guns, affairs, his mother a murderer.

"She was sick. I know it's no excuse, but she's locked away."

We normally don't have any members locked away. We have our own punishments. But I'm glad she's locked away. At least she can't hurt anyone else.

"Do you want me to continue?" I can see Lucas is toying with what to tell me. My mind is screaming no, but I find myself nodding.

"Just before you all arrived, we had a member die. He was having an affair with Henry."

I exhale loudly. Henry's gay? But my mind springs back to the idea that someone else died.

"When you say died..."

"I mean murdered."

I sit back in the seat and swallow. "Do you know who killed him?"

"Henry is blaming George."

I'm sitting up again. "George, the butler?" I ask.

Lucas nods. "I don't know if it's true."

"Did you ask him?"

Lucas breaks eye contact for the first time. "No."

I remember the day in the gardens, when Lucas had smashed my heart, and I saw George talking to a blonde lady. My stomach twists.

Does it really matter? She could have been someone who works there. But I hadn't seen her before, and she didn't look like someone who got her hands dirty.

"You're frowning." Lucas trails his finger between my eyes, and I stop frowning.

"I saw George in the gardens talking to a blonde woman." I'm remembering the moment. "I was crying, and they looked in my direction, and then both of them disappeared."

I glance up at Lucas now. "You had arrived. That's what scared them off."

CHAPTER NINE

LUCAS

My mother is blonde. My heart bounces around my chest, and I get a sickening feeling in my stomach.

"Did you see her eyes?"

Ella frowns again, and I'm tempted to kiss her, but I don't. I want her to focus.

She shrugs. "I couldn't see her eye color, but she was pretty." She chews her lip. "Her nails were painted red."

My stomach twists. My mother always painted her nails red. But that doesn't mean it was definitely her. Would I recognize her after all these years?

Fear and worry are clouding Ella's eyes, and she's suffered enough. When that man had pulled a gun on her, I didn't want to run. I had never wanted to hurt someone so badly. I will meet him again and he will pay.

I tighten my fists now. I'm twisting with an anger I still haven't released.

"I'm sorry I'm not more helpful." Ella chews her lips.

I relax my hands. "You have been." I force a smile and she relaxes, her green eyes widening. I want to take all the badness away, but I also want Ella to understand the danger. She's too naïve to how this world works, I see that now. She doesn't understand the real danger here.

"We have somewhere to go and try to figure out what we're doing."

I finally got a message from George with a name and address of the person who could help us. I don't know anything about him or how he could help us, but right now, it's all we have.

"Where are we going?"

A part of me doesn't want to tell her. What if she has another crazy idea and reveals where we are? But I can't hide all the road signs from her.

"Clifton."

Her eyes widen. "That's really far away." I can see the wheels turning in her head.

She's staring at me with watery eyes, and I know she's thinking of Hannah.

I want to tell her the truth, but I also can't bear the look in her eyes. "All the girls were sent home," I say.

She blinks rapidly. "What? When?"

"I found out yesterday."

Her mouth hangs open. "And you're only telling me now?"

I grit my teeth. "I had other things on my mind."

She bristles and sits back in the seat. Her little hands are tightened into fists. "You need to tell me things like that." She glares at me.

Guilt tries to worm its way into my heart, but I swat it aside. I'm doing this for her.

"In the future, I will." I hope.I never have to lie to her again. I can see the weight being dragged off her shoulders, so the lie is worth its weight in gold.

"I need to go to the bathroom," I tell Ella while glancing up and down the aisles before looking back at her.

"You should go, then."

Her tone has me grinning, and I stand. She looks surprised when I reach in and pull her up with me. "You have to come too."

"We're on a train. I'm not going anywhere." She rolls her eyes, and it makes me drag her behind me. She keeps proving to me that she either isn't taking in how serious this is, or I haven't driven my point home.

"I'm not worried about you going anywhere," I say as we move into another car. I don't like how many people are in here. It's packed and the heat is sweltering. We move through it quickly, and with everyone who glances at us, I assess the danger level.

The bathrooms are in the next car, and I get a few strange looks as I pull Ella into the cubicle with me. There's no space and we move around each other.

"This really isn't necessary." Ella's eyes bounce around the small space. It's not clean and I relieve myself quickly. I don't want her standing in a urine-soaked box.

We leave and Ella pauses at the ladies' room. "You aren't coming in with me."

I grin. "I'll stand at the door." She hurries in, and I keep my back to the door. A few people keep glancing my way, but when their eyes meet mine, they quickly look away.

The door hits my back, and I step away as Ella emerges. We make our way back to our seats, and I can't relax at all. Everyone who watches us could be spying for my father. Each male who runs their eyes along Ella's body gets a death glare until they promptly look away from her. She's oblivious to their stares. She's oblivious to her beauty.

I let her in first and box her in along the window. I tell myself to give her some space, but an inch away from her is an inch too much. A red timer above the door tells us we will reach Clifton in thirty minutes.

My stomach twists again. I have no idea what this Asher man is like. I glance up as a guy in a suit slides into the seat across from me and Ella. I sit up straighter as he places his paper onto the table. He looks up and smiles at Ella. I want to pull him across the table and hurt him. When his eyes land on me, he flinches and looks away.

"Go find somewhere else to sit," I say.

His head snaps up, and he takes a quick look at Ella before looking back at me.

"Now," I warn, and he gets up and gathers his newspaper.

"Jesus, Lucas. You think he's one of them?" Ella asks once the man has passed us.

"What?" I glance at Ella and take her hand in mine.

"You think he's one of the people following us?"

No, he isn't. I just didn't like how he looked at Ella.

"No," I answer honestly.

I glance down at her, and she frowns. "Why were you so rude? He seemed nice."

My stomach dives. "I just think we should treat everyone like a suspect," I say to her, and she bobs her head.

We remain silent until the train slows down at the platform. It turns from a blur to a collection of people. I get out of the seat and pull Ella with me. She doesn't complain about being dragged around the place.

We approach a cab rank, and I give him the address. Ella stares out the window as we leave the town and enter the countryside. Trees give way to mountains, and the cab driver pulls in at the mouth of a park.

I pay him, and we climb out.

"This is a park," Ella says. It's getting dark, and we still have to walk. I don't want the taxi to bring us directly to Asher. The warning in the message is that it's a safe house—from what, I'm not sure. I'm assuming for people like Asher and me.

We walk along the road. Two cars pass us, and each time, I move Ella in along the bank and block her with my body. It's instinctive, and she moves each time I direct her.

We reach a lane. A white rusted post box has the gold numbers peeling off, but I can still read them: 2242.

"This man is going to help us, but that doesn't mean we should trust him." I glance at Ella and hate the fear that's in her eyes. I stop walking and so does Ella.

"I won't let anything happen to you." I take her face in my hands. She's dangerously beautiful. I don't think she has any idea how lethal she is to my heart.

"No matter what, I will always protect you." I enforce each word, and she nods up at me. She has no idea how far I would go, who I would sacrifice for her. But that's okay.

I kiss her softly, and my body responds to the feel of her in my hands and her smell. Every cell in my body recognizes Ella. I continue walking until a large two-story cabin comes into view.

I tighten my hold on her fingers but loosen my grip when I feel her tense.

I take the five steps up onto the porch when the door opens. A blond-haired man with a full beard opens the door and nods at me. I try not to pull Ella away as his eyes flicker to her. It's quick before they return to me.

"Lucas O'Faolain," he says while opening the door for us to enter. He's glancing over us, out into the mass of earth.

"We weren't followed," I say, but he still glares out as we step into a large living space that's lit by lamps I spot in each corner of the room.

"I'm Asher." He closes the door and faces me.

"George told me."

He looks to Ella again, and his eyes soften. "Ella O'Leary," he greets her, and I don't like how he's using our full titles.

"I know you must have a lot of questions, but I'm sure that can all wait until tomorrow." He's right. I'm exhausted, and I'm sure Ella is too.

He moves. "I'll show you to your rooms. I didn't get much in, as your arrival was last minute. But I managed to get some old clothes I had stored in the attic." He stops at a door and opens it. The room is clean. A bed is made up with a stack of female clothes on it.

"Ella can stay here." He moves further down, but I hold firm.

"Ella stays with me."

He doesn't seem put out by my tone. His eyes move across me and to Ella.

"Yes, I'd like to stay with Lucas." Her voice sounds so timid.

Asher nods at her. "This way."

He has gained a bit more of my respect for allowing Ella to make the decision of whether she's staying with me or not.

If she had said no, it wouldn't have really mattered. She's staying in the same room as I am. He opens the door to a larger room, and I see clothes stacked on a trunk.

"I'll get Ella's clothes." He leaves as we step into the room. Ella looks nervous, and I don't want that.

"I'll sleep on the floor. I just want us in the same room."

She shakes her head. "No, we can get some extra pillows." She won't look at me.

Asher arrives back with Ella's clothes.

"Could we have some extra pillows?" Ella asks sweetly, and I move around the room. My mind won't settle.

"Sure." Asher leaves again, and I kick off my shoes. He arrives back with a stack of pillows.

"I wasn't sure how many you needed." He places them on a chair that has a throw across the back of it.

"That's great." Ella's sweet voice has me gritting my teeth. I'm irritated with everything, and her being nice to Asher is testing my barriers.

I want to tell Asher to leave. His eyes dart to me. "We'll talk tomorrow."

I nod, and he leaves. Once the door is closed, I feel for the first time that I can breathe.

CHAPTER TEN

ELLA

My heart pumps harder the more I stare at the bed. So much has happened, and all I can think about is Lucas. Someone needs to slap me. He has so much to worry about, but all I want is to have his hands on me.

I remove my shoes and pink socks. After pushing the socks inside my sneakers, I place them under the chair that holds a mountain of pillows. I don't want them between me and Lucas, but I'm trying to look like I have some control.

I pick up the clothes that Asher left for me. They're old-fashioned—a long white shirt with light blue stripes, a pair of beige pants that look way too big. Another pair of trousers that look better fitting and a stack of woolen jumpers.

No night garments are amongst the stack. I glance at Lucas, who's watching me, and I can't read the look on his face. I feel embarrassed about assessing clothes while we're in this situation. It should be the last thing on my mind.

"I don't have nightclothes," I babble, and I internally roll my eyes at myself.

What I don't expect is for Lucas to take off his black T-shirt and hand it to me.

"You can wear my top."

I swallow as I stare at his tanned, toned chest. He's chiseled and carved by the hands of God. No one else could make such perfection. I can't look away as I stretch out my hand and gauge where the T-shirt is. My fist circles around the fabric.

"Thanks." I peel my eyes away from him and turn around. There isn't an en suite in the room, so I have nowhere to change. Keeping my back to Lucas, I pull the soft black jumper over my head and quickly pull down his T-shirt. Lucas shifts and I glance at him. He has his back to me, his hands balled into fists as he drags the curtains closed.

I shimmy out of my jeans. The T-shirt sits above my knees. When he has the curtains closed, his eyes clash with mine. The darkness swirls and expands, and my core tightens. I try to calm my racing heart by gathering all six pillows and throwing them onto the bed. Pulling back the blanket, I place one in between us. Then I place a second on top of the first before smashing down a third. I still have three more, so I place them below the first stack.

"Are you building a wall?" I can hear the humor in Lucas's growl.

I rise on my knees to see him and regret it. He climbs up onto the bed, and I swallow as he plucks the top pillow away, revealing more of his stomach. When he removes the second one, my eyes dip lower to the *V* that disappears into black boxers. He isn't wearing trousers. I nod as I try to keep calm. His hand is on the final pillow.

Once again, he's giving me an option. My heart kicks around inside my chest.

"Did I tell you that black is my favorite color?"

I fist his T-shirt at the belly before peeling my eyes away from his muscled chest and then make my way back up to his inky eyes. My heart thuds.

"Yes." I sound breathless. I want to ask him if he can see what he's doing to me with just a look. The emotions he drags up in me are terrifying. I never knew someone could hijack your system. I shuffle forward and reach for his shoulders. His skin is warm, and it sends electricity shooting through me.

He's a solid mass under my fingertips. His erection brushes my stomach, and I can feel everything in me blooming and pushing to the surface. My breasts grow heavy. Inside my bra, I can feel my nipples harden. My lips touch his, and I chance a look at him. He's as still as a statue, but his eyes are so alive.

I have no idea what's going through his head. I pull back from him in case this isn't why he was removing the pillows. His erection is giving me one signal, but his eyes are telling me a different story.

The last pillow sails through the air, and I'm on my back. His lips come down heavily on mine, and I can't match his ferocity as he deepens the kiss with his tongue. His hands touch everywhere, and I'm a jumble of nerves and groans. It's all too much; it's not enough.

My skin feels clammy, and I manage to get out from under him and pull off the T-shirt. His eyes drink me up, and when his wet lips part, I know I want them in hidden places.

Tasting me, licking me.

My core tightens as he reaches for me, and I'm under him again. He spreads my legs and holds himself between them. His kisses are tinged with a savagery that lessens, until each kiss becomes tender and sears me. He doesn't speak as he continues his assault on my heart, as he presses small kisses to my lips. His hands aren't roaming, but our bodies are flushed together. His shaft feels so heavy on my stomach. It excites me and also makes me nervous. The first time having him inside me was painful—more than I could have imagined.

He leans up, leaving a final kiss on my lips. My heart starts a new beat, one that I now associate with Lucas. It's wild, like I'm at the top of a roller coaster and waiting to fall. It's exciting and terrifying all rolled into one.

He pushes down his boxers, and his cock springs out. I swallow. It's big. So big. He takes the boxers off, and when he crawls halfway back up me and pulls at the band of my panties, I'm barely containing myself. It feels painfully slow as he drags them off me before he moves back up.

My legs part for him, and his cock sits at my entrance. I'm waiting for him to return to kissing me. I want his lips on mine, but he doesn't. He pushes himself inside me and fills me, stretching my tunnel. I wrap around him like we were made for each other. He's holding himself up as he stares down at me, moving in and out. This time, there's the smallest of pain, but the pleasure that's filling me up is like nothing I've experienced. I have nothing to compare it to; only, I will compare everything to this.

Tears brim at the surface as my emotions heighten. The ecstasy on Lucas's face as he moves in and out of me is my focus, my anchor to the emotions that swim below the surface, ready to break free. Everything is moving faster inside, clawing at me. Lucas goes faster, but his eyes are so soft as he holds me captive. I can't think. I can only feel as his pace quickens, and I'm all wrapped up in Lucas and his love, and it's too much. Everything in me wants to break free, and I want to cry out my love as my world shatters and I call out his name. I turn my head as lights flare and die while I come down off the high. Tears leak from my eyes, and I have no idea what's happening. Lucas has slowed. His own high tips over the same time as mine. The air is thin, and I take in ragged breaths.

Lucas touches my face, and I glance at him. He freezes above me.

"Did I hurt you?"

I'm shaking my head. "No, not at all."

He touches a tear.

"I don't know." I half laugh, unable to explain why it all felt like too much.

He isn't happy, and I don't want him to think he did anything wrong. He did everything so right.

"I think it's like when you laugh so much, and you start to cry." I can feel my lips tug down, and I'm overwhelmed with emotion. It's Lucas. It's us running. It's everything that's happened.

Lucas still holds me with his stare. He's searching my face, and I can see he isn't satisfied. I reach up and press my lips to his. He has to know how I feel. His cock twitches inside me, and I pull away.

He doesn't shy away but grins. "The things you do to me."

He makes me feel powerful with how he looks at me. I want to tell him that he has weakened me, and I'd do anything for him.

He slowly takes himself out and lifts himself so he's beside me. I feel the loss for a moment before he pulls me into his arms and squashes our bodies together. His lips brush the crown of my head, and I soak up the feeling of warmth and love.

I lie in his arms and fall asleep smiling.

***

I wake up still in Lucas's arms. He's sound asleep as I slowly and carefully detangle myself from him. I get dressed into my own jeans and one of the wooly jumpers that Asher left out for me. I don't bother with socks or shoes as I creep from the room and pad softly down the hall, opening doors as I go. I find the bathroom and relieve my bladder. Two new toothbrushes still in the wrappers sit on a small glass shelf below the mirror. I open one and brush my teeth before washing my face. I feel fresh. It's the first time in a long time I've slept properly.

The living room is basking in the morning light. It's early. The sun has only set, and as I step up to a large window, I stare out at a white world.

It's snowing.

Lucas is still asleep when I return to the room and get my socks and sneakers. I close the door quietly behind me and slip them on in the living room before going outside.

I'm careful as I walk down the steps—the last two are coated in snow. Once my feet sink into the white carpet, I wrap my arms around myself. It's cold, but it's peaceful. Something magical swirls in the air, and I want to take it in. Large, thin green trees rise high into the surrounding sky. The park we stopped at is forested, and I can see the tops of all the trees in the distance. They seem endless.

The door behind me creaks open, and I glance over my shoulder as Lucas's sleepy head pops out the door.

"Go inside, you'll get cold." My stomach flips as he runs his hands through his tousled hair. He's in the black T-shirt again, and he's divine.

"What are you doing?" He stretches as he walks to me, and I see tanned skin peeking out.

"I love the snow," I say as I focus on his smiling lips.

"You can admire it from inside." He reaches me and wraps his arms around my waist. "Where it's warm."

"I like it out here," I say as he distracts me with a kiss to my nose.

"You don't feel a bit bad that I'm freezing to death?"

A laugh rumbles through me. "You only just came out. Go inside, you big baby."

He pulls me closer, and my body hums. He presses a kiss to my jawline, and I close my eyes to his warmth. The coldness of the air around us is making his closeness a cocoon I want to bury myself in.

He starts to hum while we move in a tiny circle. I'm smiling into his neck.

"What are you doing?" I ask slowly.

He stops humming. "Attempting to sing to you."

I laugh again, and he leans out so I can see him. He's smiling. We still move in a small circle.

"Isn't this in one of your fairy tales? The prince dances with the princess in the snow." He raises a brow.

I bite my lip to keep in more laughter. "No."

He surprises me with another kiss to my nose. "Maybe I'm just trying to keep warm." His eyes dance with a lightness I haven't seen before. I don't want it to go away.

"Sing to me."

He pulls me back into his neck, and he hums out of key. It sounds like a distorted version of *Rock-A-bye Baby*, but I'm not sure. It's perfect, and I close my eyes as we dance in the same spot until the snow turns slushy under our feet.

"Maybe we could buy a holiday home up here, since you like the snow so much."

I move out and glance up at Lucas. My heart bounces around in my chest. He's talking about the future with me.

I bite the inside of my jaw as I'm overwhelmed with a need to cry. What is wrong with me?

"That sounds lovely," I manage to squeeze out.

"But?" Lucas's brows draw down, and I hate that I've dampened the mood.

I shake my head. "We need to fix all this first." I chew the inside of my jaw again. I can't ignore how the world around us is falling apart.

"I will." Lucas's serious tone has me reaching up and touching his face. "No, Lucas, we will." I'm not allowing him to do this alone.

"Let's go inside." He takes my hand from his face and entwines our fingers together. I nod, allowing this conversation to die, but he needs to understand that we're in this together.

Asher is in the kitchen. It's open-plan, situated on the back of the living room. Lucas goes back to the bedroom to get a jumper, so I feel self-conscious entering the kitchen area.

"You have a beautiful home," I say while pulling the sleeves of the cream jumper down over my freezing hands. His eyes roam across me, and I see pain flicker across his face.

"Thank you, Ella."

His stare is intense, and I feel uncomfortable. He must notice as he turns to the pan and removes some rashers from it. "Sorry for staring." There's something familiar about his soft blue eyes, but I can't put my finger on it.

"The jumper was my wife's."

I hate the word "was." Am I wearing a dead person's clothes? I want to pull it off, but I hold still. Lucas enters the kitchen, and his eyes narrow as he glares at Asher.

"It's very warm." I can't think of anything else to say. His smile is hidden behind a blond beard, which in the light showcases some gray.

"Breakfast is ready." He adds two rashers to a plate with an egg and toast on it and walks over to a large oak table that's been set for three. Lucas brushes a kiss to my forehead as he leads me to the table. Asher keeps taking peeks at us, and he looks amused.

Lucas pulls out my chair, and when I look up to thank him, he's glaring at Asher. I have no idea why he's being so hostile.

"Thank you," I say as Asher places a plate in front of me before bringing over a pot of tea. Lucas is the last to sit. He's picked the head of the table, with me on his left and Asher on his right. I'm sure that was Asher's seat, but he doesn't say anything.

"I hope you slept well." Asher looks up at me through bites, and I can feel my cheeks heat. Oh God. Did he hear us? I'm being paranoid.

"Why are you in a safe house?"

My mouth hangs open as Lucas speaks gruffly. Asher has been kind to us, but Lucas is treating him like a suspect. I don't want to be kicked out.

"I'm hiding just like you." Asher isn't put out at all by Lucas's demeanor.

"How long have you been in hiding?" I notice that Lucas hasn't touched his food. His hands sit on either side of his plate, fisted.

I want to touch him so he relaxes, but I don't.

"Nearly thirty years."

The fork clatters against my plate. "I'm sorry." I pick it up and try to smile through my apology. "It's just such a long time." *Thirty years.*

"It is a long time," Asher says with sadness clouding his eyes. His soft words make me feel for him.

"Are you here alone?" I ask. He said this had been his wife's jumper—past tense. Does that mean she's dead?

"Yes. I do have visitors the odd time."

"What are you hiding from?" Lucas asks, and I want to know too. My heart drums as Asher focuses on his food.

"It isn't my place to tell you. George will be arriving today, and he can inform you."

The chair scrapes as Lucas stands and bends over the table. "You will tell me now." He's in Asher's face, and my heart pangs.

I reach out and touch his arm. "Lucas, please." I don't want him to hurt Asher. I want answers too, but not like this.

My touch has the desired effect, and he sits back in his seat. Asher glances at me again with a look of thanks in his eyes. I feel like I've betrayed Lucas, so I focus on my plate.

"Did you decorate the place yourself?" I ask, hoping to steer us to softer ground.

I can feel Lucas's eyes bore into me, and I take a peek at him. Yep, he's pretty angry.

"Eat." The pleading note in my voice has him exhaling heavily, and he picks up his knife and fork. He might be eating, but he's back to interrogating Asher.

"Who are you hiding from?"

I'm ready to leave the table when Asher speaks.

"Your father."

CHAPTER ELEVEN

LUCAS

"**M**aster Andrew." Ella's stunned voice has me glancing at her. I clench my jaw when I see the fear in her eyes.

"You have been hiding from my father for thirty years?" The disbelief I feel is echoed in my words.

Asher grates on my nerves as he cuts into his egg. He keeps glancing at Ella, and I want to hurt him. I'm not touching him, because I don't want to upset Ella. He should be thanking her.

"Why?" I quiz, and he glances at me from the corner of his eye. "You are in my home, Lucas. I haven't asked you one question. So I don't appreciate being interrogated."

Ella's so tense beside me and has stopped eating. I want to smash his fucking face in. I force a smile. "You are right. Let's eat."

He's not buying my lie, and I hope he reads my face loud and clear—I'm letting this go for now. I glance at Ella, and her eyes ping-pong from me to Asher.

"Eat your breakfast," I tell her, and she forks some egg into her mouth. Staring at her calms me, and for her, I hold it together.

"Why don't you tell Ella about who decorated your home, Asher."

I grind out the words, and he accepts the pass and smiles at Ella. She relaxes further as he tells her he's the decorator. She compliments his home while I think of how I'm going to extract the information from him without alerting Ella. As the last forkful of my dinner enters my mouth, Ella glances at my plate. Each time I eat, she seems happier.

When the plates are cleared, I glare at Asher. His time is up. He knows it; I see it in his eyes.

"You can go check out upstairs if you want. One of the rooms has lots of clothes you can go through and pick out what you want."

"No, I couldn't do that." Ella looks shyly away, and I take an internal breath before taking her hand.

"Go have a look. You need more warm clothes."

Her eyes flicker to Asher. "We're only going to have a boy chat." She's gnawing her lip, and I don't want her to worry. But she's unconvinced.

"Ella, everything is okay," I tell her.

"Lucas is right, we're just going to talk." Asher foolishly backs me up, and it's the deciding factor for Ella as she pushes out her chair.

"Okay, I'll take a look." She keeps glancing back as she leaves the room.

I look to Asher, dropping all pretenses.

"I know who you are, Lucas, and I know the things you've done. I know what you're capable of. But me telling you things without George will only confuse the matter. I'm asking you to give me a few hours, and when George gets here, we'll explain everything." He isn't begging; he's asking. And a part of me respects that.

It's a small part, and none of this is sitting right with me. I've walked into a situation trusting George, and now I have to trust this stranger. If it was just me, I think I could. But Ella is upstairs, oblivious to how dangerous this situation really is.

"Do you have a laundry room?" I ask.

His brows draw down in confusion. "Yes, why?" he asks, but I'm standing.

"Show me." He rises, and irritation tightens the corners of his eyes, but he walks to the back of the kitchen and opens a small door. I lean in. It's a small room with a washer and dryer. This will work.

I push Asher in, and he turns to protest. I don't hold back as my fist collides with his nose. He reels back, and I close the door behind us before hitting the dials on the dryer. It kicks in immediately. Asher isn't howling in pain, but he holds his face as he looks up at me.

"Why are you hiding from my father?"

Asher shakes his head, and my fist rams into his stomach. He doubles over and lands on the ground.

"Just tell me now and this ends."

Asher looks up at me, and I grind my teeth. He's smiling while he wipes blood from his nose.

"You are a bigger asshole than they told me you would be."

I close the distance. "Who?"

"George."

I grip his throat. "You said they? Not singular, but plural?"

I give him a warning glare.

"Lucas, Asher." Ella's soft voice passes by the door, and I tighten my hold on Asher's throat.

"Lucas." She sounds panicked, but her voice trails away.

I release Asher and leave the laundry room. Walking around the counter, she spins in the living room and she half smiles with relief.

"Where were you?" She's looking behind me for Asher.

"Here." I reach her. "Did you find some clothes?" I ask.

She's glancing behind me again. "Where's Asher?"

I hear the accusation there.

"Doing laundry."

She peeks over my shoulder and relaxes. We can hear the rumble of the dryer. "The clothes are nice," she says.

I pull her in closer to me. "You want to show me?"

She smiles, and I let her lead the way. I glance back at the kitchen, but Asher hasn't come out of the laundry room.

Upstairs is a hallway of doors. I'm curious what's behind them all.

"In here." Ella stands in a room that's filled with boxes. Her green eyes are wide with wonder as she glances around the space.

"So many treasures."

I love the way she views things. All I see is rubbish where she sees treasure.

She sits down cross-legged and continues pulling clothes out of a box.

I open a few beside me but don't go through its contents. It's only clothes and more clothes. I move around the room. A brown teddy sticks out of a box at the back of the space. I reach in and pull it out. It's missing an eye. I glance into the box of toys, old toys.

"He must have had a child," I say and glance over at Ella. She pauses in her search, and her eyes are filled with sadness.

"Or maybe these were his," I say, wanting to erase the sadness.

She shakes her head. "No, I think something bad happened to his family. I think his wife is dead." She looks back at an ugly orange shirt in her hands. "I think all this is his wife's."

She looks so sad, her green eyes swimming with that asshole's loss. "I can't see anyone marrying him."

She tilts her head. "He seems nice, Lucas." She's pleading again, and I drop the subject.

I put the teddy back into the box, the light glinting off a picture. I take it out, and my stomach hollows. I recognize Asher. He doesn't have a beard, but his blond hair and blue eyes are the same. A woman looks up at him, smiling, deep brown eyes wide and staring adoringly at him.

Beside her is my father. He's staring straight at the camera like he's looking at me now. It's unnerving. I swallow and my anger ignites as big blue eyes stare at me. Blonde hair falls across my mother's shoulders. She's smiling at the camera, and she looks so young, so carefree. My hand grips the frame, my thumbs digging into the glass.

My heart beats wildly, and she's exactly as I remember her. Her red nails rest against the white dress that flows around her. The glass cracks under my hand.

"Lucas, what did you find?" Ella moves behind me, and I drop the picture, emotions choking me.

"Nothing." I close my eyes against the waves of anger.

I can hear the creak of the floorboards, and I turn as Asher appears in the doorway. He's holding a rag to his face. His neck is red raw, and Ella's sharp inhale has me wanting to throttle him.

"What happened?" She sounds shocked.

"Your boyfriend attacked me."

I smirk at Asher's brazen words. Ella's staring at me for answers, but I'm too twisted with anger.

"You know my parents." I'm walking to him, and for the first time his eyes widen with fear.

"I'm done playing games." I reach him and force him back to the banister. He looks behind him, his face paling.

"Who are you?" I roar all my anger.

"Lucas, please." Ella's breathless beside us, and I can't look at her right now.

"Go downstairs," I order her and shake Asher. "Tell me now." I push half of his body over the banister.

Ella screams, but I focus on Asher. "Who are you?" I say it calmer and loosen my hold on him.

"I'm Asher Bradley, a member of the committee. Let me up now." He's scrambling.

I'm shocked and pull him away from the banister. I release him, and he quickly takes several steps away from me while rubbing his neck.

"I want you out of my home, now." He's shouting as he walks away from me.

He's Alex's father. His wife is Sorcha. Why did George send me here?

"What is wrong with you?" Ella's outburst snaps me out of my shock.

She looks ready to pass out.

"Calm down." I take a step toward her, and she takes two back while shaking her head.

"I don't know you when you become that." She's pointing at the banister. "I don't recognize you when you hurt people."

Her lip trembles, and I try to find the calm in me but I can't.

"Calm down," I repeat for both of us.

Ella shakes her head. "You're scaring me." It's whispered but she may as well be roaring it at the top of her lungs. Her words cut so deep, and I can't stand here and have her judge me. Not her.

I turn away as I try to reel in the anger and pain that churns inside me. I return to the room and take the picture out of the box. I pull the frame apart and take out the picture. I return to Ella, who hasn't moved.

"You told me you saw a blonde woman talking to George." I show her the picture and point at my mother.

I push the picture closer so she can get a good look.

She stares at the picture, then her eyes jump up to me.

"Ella, is that her?" My voice is too loud, but I need to know.

She nods her head. "Yes."

CHAPTER TWELVE

ELLA

Lucas races from the house, but I can't move. I've never seen him so angry, so pained. My heart beats wildly in my chest as I think about the raw look of pain on his face.

Asher told us to leave. We have nowhere to go. I find him in the kitchen with an ice pack on his neck.

He glares at me, and I know I should leave the room, but I don't know where to go.

"I'm sorry," I start with, and he glares at me again without speaking. At least he isn't shouting at me to leave. My heart sinks when I think of the look of devastation on Lucas's face.

"He's a good person," I tell Asher.

"You have no idea who he really is. What lurks under the surface. He's vicious. Just like his father."

I tighten my fists. "That's not true. You don't know him. His father is a monster. He made him..."

Asher moves the ice pack to the other side of his neck. I try not to look at the marks as I convince this man to let us stay.

"My son has told me the type of man he is, and it's not a nice one." Asher's eyes soften. "You are a lovely girl, Ella. You deserve better."

I ignore his remark. "Please don't kick us out. We have nowhere to go."

"He's not coming back into my home. You are welcome, but not him."

I shake my head. "Please."

"When George arrives, he can figure out where he stays. But it won't be here."

My throat burns as Asher walks past me. I turn and look out the large window that looks out onto the expanse of white. I spot Lucas. He's squatting at the tree line, and the pain I feel seeing him is like pain I've never known.

I love him. But I'm afraid to go to him. I cover my mouth with my hands as I allow myself to keep him in my sights. The pain swallows me. How quickly things can change.

His anger has him rising and stomping into the tree line. My heart pounds and claws its way up my throat. I'm shaking my head.

"Don't leave me," I whisper to the glass. He pauses as if he heard me, but that's not possible. I feel crushed as he walks into the forest.

I'm moving. I burst from the back door and I'm running, tearing up the snow under my feet.

"Don't leave me," I shout as panic claws at me. "Lucas! Don't leave me!"

I can't stop the onslaught of pain that tears through my system at the idea of him leaving.

"Don't leave me." He turns, and I don't stop until I'm in his arms. He doesn't hug me back.

"Don't leave me." I'm crying too much, but I can't keep it together. He's my safety and I can't lose it.

I feel like I can't breathe as I cling to him. His arms move around me.

"I love you." I sob into his shirt. "Don't leave me," I whisper again as I unfold in his arms.

"I would never leave you." He tightens his hold on me. His words have me clinging tighter to him, sobbing harder.

"Jesus, Ella. It's okay." He's rubbing my back, my hair. "It's okay. I would never leave you." His words soothe some of my pain.

"You're the reason I'm here." He kisses the crown of my head.

"It's okay."

I keep my head buried in his neck, soaking him with pain that lessens when his words sink in. *He wasn't leaving*, I tell myself as he continues to run his hands across my back.

"I would never leave you." His words are like concrete set around my heart. My sobs subside, and I start to come to the surface, aware of the biting cold along my back.

The idea of Lucas leaving is too much. I know I love him, but this is deeper than love.

His hands leave my back and hold my forearms. "Ella, look at me." The softness in his voice has me raising wet lashes as I lean out.

A ghost of a smile haunts his eyes but doesn't fully materialize. "I will never leave you."

I'm nodding at each word he says clearly.

He tucks a piece of hair behind my ear. His eyes are troubled. "I'm sorry about what just happened. I shouldn't have threatened Asher."

I don't think he really means that he's sorry for threatening Asher. It sounds more like he's sorry I witnessed it.

"He won't let you back in." My voice wavers with a new rise of grief. Where will we go?

"I'll fix it," he says before pulling me back into his arms.

"I'll fix all of it."

His promise is spoken into my hair, and I allow myself to exist within this moment with Lucas, surrounded by his warmth, tall trees, and a blanket of snow.

"Let's get back. You're freezing," he says.

I am, but leaving Lucas has me tightening my hold on him.

His laugh rumbles through me. "I'm not going anywhere, Ella."

I glance up at him and bob my head. "Okay."

It feels like a longer walk back to the house. Lucas entwines our fingers together, and I can't stop taking peeks at him as the white world seems to float around us. He's wearing all black, and he looks dangerous and forbidding. His eyes clash with mine, and I smile at him. I'm still a bit raw, but each step we take pieces me a little more back together.

"I've already asked Asher to let you in. I can't see him budging."

Lucas squeezes our entwined fingers. "I can be quite charming when I want to be."

I laugh. "You're going to charm Asher?" I can't get rid of the smile that's plastered itself to my face.

We reach the steps of the cabin.

"You go in and warm up, and I'll start rehearsing my lines."

My stomach twists at leaving him out here.

"You can make me a coffee while you're in there."

I know what he's doing—giving me a job to do so I won't think about him being out here in the freezing cold. I lean in and kiss his cheek gently.

"How many sugars?"

His eyes smile at me. "Two."

I hate going inside, but the warmth reminds me how cold it is outside. Asher's back in the kitchen, and I feel more determined now.

"He's freezing out there," I say as I step into the kitchen.

Asher glances at me but doesn't say anything. It's clear in his eyes. He isn't bending.

I want to keep explaining, but maybe allowing Lucas to use his charm could be more effective.

"Is it okay if I make a coffee?"

"Is it for you?" Asher rubs his neck, which is starting to look bruised.

I focus on his eyes. "Yes."

He nods and steps past me. "Then go ahead."

I fill up the kettle and get it on before returning to the window. I can't see Lucas from this angle, and that makes me nervous. The kettle takes what feels like hours to boil, and when it finally clicks, I nearly burn my hand in my haste to make us coffee.

Lucas glances up as I open the door while holding both coffees in one hand.

He clears the steps and takes them out of my hand.

"Thanks," I say, pulling the door closed behind me. I don't want Asher to see me with two mugs.

Lucas holds up two mugs. "Which one?"

"It doesn't matter. I made them the exact same."

He hands me the red mug, and I smile into the hot contents. I'm not much of a coffee drinker, but I want to taste it because Lucas likes it.

"How is your rehearsal going?" I ask as I step up to the wooden railing that encloses the porch. At least we have shelter here.

Lucas glances at me before taking a drink of his coffee. He's a head taller than me as I stand beside him.

I hear the sound of a vehicle at the same time Lucas does, and my heart slams against my chest. They've found us. We're caught.

"Stay here." Lucas places the cup on the edge of the rail before moving down the steps. As he passes me, he gives me a look that tells me not to move. He walks around the side of the cabin and disappears.

The coffee turns sour in my stomach as I wait. Has he been gone too long? I'm ready to move, when Lucas reappears, and beside him is George. Relief has me smiling, but it's short-lived when I notice how tight Lucas's face is.

George looks up at me. "Lady Ella." His soft words have me smiling. He isn't wearing his black clothing like I'm used to seeing him in. His brown cords and dark gray jumper make him look even friendlier. Like he's someone's grandfather.

"Hi, George." He climbs the steps onto the porch while rubbing his hands together. "It's cold up here," he says, looking out onto the expanse of white. Lucas joins us, and he's scowling, but he doesn't say anything. George seems relaxed, like he's home.

"It's beautiful," I say while I take a much-needed sip of my coffee.

When I look at George, he's smiling. "It is. I've always had a fondness for the snow."

Lucas clears his throat, and George looks away. "I think it's best we all go in."

I turn to Lucas to hear how he's going to explain this one.

He moves past George and picks up his coffee. "After you, George."

My mouth opens to tell Lucas that it isn't fair, sending George in first.

"Come on, Ella." There's a smile in his voice as he waits for me to follow after George. I do and hope Asher doesn't completely lose it. Lucas closes the door behind us.

I hear voices. Asher isn't alone. It's a voice I recognize. My heart pounds a little harder as George, Lucas, and I step into the living space. Asher is smiling, his arms spread wide as Alex steps into his embrace.

It's his father—the blue eyes and softness that are so familiar to me. Asher and Alex hug briefly before they separate and look up. Alex's eyes ping across everyone until they land on me. He isn't wearing his usual attire. He looks normal in jeans and a navy jumper.

"Ella." He says my name like we're old friends.

I return the smile. "Hi, Alex." This is weird, how everyone is staying quiet. I don't dare look at Lucas. I can feel the waves of anger pouring off him. Maybe everyone else can, too. Asher's eyes snap to Lucas's before they narrow on George.

"He is not welcome in my home, George. He attacked me."

Alex steps forward as he glares at Lucas.

"He wasn't forthcoming with information." Lucas's words drip with anger. So much for him being charming. This is a train wreck.

"Get out!" I jump at Asher's raised voice.

"Asher, we need him." George breaks away from us and walks to Asher. They must have a conversation with their eyes. By the time George reaches Asher, he's calmer.

"I want him to keep his distance from me," Asher tells George while glowering at Lucas. I glance at Lucas now, and his anger is filling his fists and tightening his jaw. I hate seeing him like this.

"He will," George reassures him.

I take a step toward Lucas, my movement grabbing his attention. I don't know what he sees on my face, but he uncurls his fists and tries to relax his frame.

"Lucas, you will keep your distance?" It's a question that's backed by a command from George.

Lucas reaches out and surprises me when he entwines our fingers together.

"I will." His answer has my body sighing in relief. I hadn't noticed how tense I was.

Asher doesn't look satisfied, and Alex's blue eyes are alive with his own outrage. It makes me think of how easily Lucas had knocked him to the ground that day in the gardens. How he had stood over him. I wonder if Alex is thinking the same thing as his eyes jump from my and Lucas's joined hands to me. He looks disappointed.

I swallow my discomfort. Lucas walks to the couch, taking me with him. "Is this the stage that someone explains to me what's going on?"

Lucas sits down and takes me with him. Once I'm tucked close to his side, he releases my hand and puts his arm across the back of the couch.

George lets out a long breath, and there's an uneasy look in his eyes as he nods at Lucas.

"Where do I start?" He sits down in a rocking chair to the left of the fireplace.

"I'd accept anywhere at this stage." I want to touch Lucas's leg to stop the rise of his irritation that will surely morph itself into anger.

"Asher, I'm sure you're wondering why Alex is here." George glances over at the kitchen area, and I follow his gaze, my stomach tightening as my eyes clash with Alex's.

I feel like Alex is judging me, and I want to explain that Lucas isn't a bad person, that we just saw a bad side of him. That he has more sides than one.

Alex looks away from me and surprisingly takes a step into the living room, then sits down across from me and Lucas. His eyes hold a challenge as he speaks to Lucas.

"Your brother locked me up and left me for dead."

Asher steps into the space. "I told you we should have taken him out sooner." Asher sounds panicked as he speaks to George, who holds his hands up.

"He's safe. I tipped off Andrew to his whereabouts, and he was released."

"He's your brother too." Lucas removes his hand from the back of the couch and moves forward in his seat. My heart is in my mouth. Alex and Henry are brothers, so that makes Alex and Lucas brothers too?

"Half brother," Alex speaks up.

Lucas tightens his fists.

Alex looks victorious as he smiles. "I've always known."

Lucas exhales loudly as he turns to George. "Do you know who he is?" I get the urge to touch Lucas again as he grinds his teeth. I'm glad he's no longer focused on Alex. I've moved without noticing and shimmy backward on the couch.

I hope George knows what he's doing. He doesn't seem threatened by Lucas. "Yes."

I don't know what passes between George and Lucas, but George tilts his head. "I could never tell you Lucas. Would you have believed me?"

I have no idea what's going on, but whatever is being confessed is life-altering for Lucas. I can feel the room hold its breath.

"Tell me why I'm here," Lucas says.

George nods like his whole life is building up to this moment. "Because you are going to help us take your father down."

I'm waiting for someone to laugh and say they're joking. What is this? But as I look from George to Alex and even Asher, I see the truth in all their eyes.

They all have one goal in common, and Lucas is the final piece.

CHAPTER THIRTEEN

LUCAS

She's the only reason I'm not reaching for George. I looked at him like a father figure. Throughout my whole life, he was always there with a soft word or a gentle touch. He never said anything, but I always felt his sadness toward me. I never really let him in, but to hear that he knew about Henry being my half brother had a sense of betrayal coursing through me.

I feel like I'm surrounded by enemies as Asher, Alex, and George watch me like I'm a ticking bomb. Ella seems so small and afraid beside me. I try to relax, to keep my cool for her sake.

"Help you? Or help the man who would be bitter with my father for sleeping with his wife? Or how about the weird boy?" I look at Alex. If he looks at Ella one more time, I'm going to lose it. He keeps peeking at her like he knows her. "You knew who Henry was but still befriended him."

"I know this is a lot to take in," George starts to plead, but I'm so ready to leave this room.

"No, George, it's not a lot to take in. I see it now. An underpaid staff member, a scorned husband." I flicker a smirk at Alex. "And him." I shrug. "What's not to get?"

"I told you he was impossible." Asher speaks up, and I know I said I would keep my distance, but I flash him a warning look not to test me.

"My father is my problem, and I fully intend to remove him myself. So I don't need"—I wave at them all—"whatever this is, as a reason. I already have one." I glance at Ella and some of my anger abates.

"Could I have a moment alone with Lucas?" George speaks to Asher, and I want to tell him not to bother.

"Why don't you go with Alex," George tells Ella with a soft smile.

Alex stands up, and when I glare at him, he's looking at Ella. "We can catch up," Alex says, and I see the fucking smirk on his face.

I'm standing and closing the distance between us. Everyone moves at once.

"Violence is not your friend, Lucas. It's your enemy, but Alex isn't the enemy here."

"Did you kill Declan?" I spin on George, so sick of his shit. I feel so betrayed.

"No." George doesn't even flinch.

"Are you going to tell me you know who did?" I ask.

"The same person who killed my wife." Asher's words are wrapped in pain and delivered with anger.

I don't feel sorry for him. I laugh. "You're pointing the finger at my mother?" I want to defend her because she can't defend herself, yet I feel angry at her too. Is she back in the house? Ella saw her talking to George.

"Ella saw you talking to my mother." My mind is a jumble.

"I was, but let me explain everything, Lucas. This won't get anyone anywhere."

"Lucas." Ella's voice is soft, and I look down at her. She has her chin held high. She does that when she's nervous but determined.

"I think George is right. You two seem like you have a lot of talking to do. Just listen to him." The pleading in her voice breaks through the cloud of anger that clings to me.

"I don't want you near Alex." I know he's right beside us, and I don't give a shit that he can hear me, but I don't want her in his vicinity.

She tilts her head, ready to argue, but I'm done bending. "No, Ella," I say before she starts.

Her eyes tighten and her cheeks redden. "I'll be in my room." I see this isn't over, but I will settle on that. I wait until she leaves the room before looking at Alex.

"You're threatened by me?" He sounds so joyous.

"Alex," George warns, but I wave George off as I take a step toward Alex.

"Put your hands on my son, and both you and Ella are gone." Asher steps up beside Alex. "Come on."

Alex drops his eyes and follows his father out of the room. I can't look back at George. I don't want to be alone with him.

"Sit down, Lucas."

I glare at him, and his eyes soften. "Please."

I sit down, but not because he said please. I don't want Ella to be on her own for long. She's already suffering enough today.

"I was a young man when I started to work for your grandfather. He took pride in his role as a leader. He was a fitting leader." I want to tell him to fast the fuck forward, but I hold still.

"When I started to work for your father, I slipped into the role as your mother's servant, not your father's, so I grew close to her."

"You had a thing for my mother?"

His laughter is genuine. "Don't let Elizabeth hear you say that. No. I respected your mother and loved her like a daughter." His smile leaves as he looks up at me. "When your father had the affair with Sorcha, it nearly destroyed her. It did, in fact, destroy both families. Asher is as much a victim here as your mother. Just like you and Alex."

I hold up my hand. "Don't compare me to him."

George wisely continues. "Your father has always kept a mistress. There were more before Sorcha, and after her." I shift uncomfortably. I hate hearing about my father's unfaithfulness.

"But Sorcha got pregnant, and Henry was the result."

"I know all that. Henry claims you hated him."

George nods. "I did. I hated everything he was at the time, and that was wrong of me, Lucas."

"Did you torture him?"

His eyes widen with surprise. "Of course not."

He seems genuine. But I don't know who to believe anymore.

"Sorcha ended the affair with your father shortly after she had Henry." His shoulders lift while he frowns. "I don't know if it was because he had no control. Maybe he loved her, who knows. But he killed her."

I'm shaking my head now. I want to tell him he's wrong, that my mother killed Sorcha and tried to kill Henry. That's why she's locked away.

"Asher has been hiding here because he witnessed it. He found your father over the body."

I'm imagining someone hurting Ella. I wouldn't hide. I'd destroy them and everyone they love.

"There was a bounty placed on Asher's head. There still is. Your father took everything from him. He took Henry and Alex. Asher was powerless to your father."

"I stood on the sidelines for years, knowing what had happened. Your father continued to abuse his power and then you arrived, the heir to his throne. I think we all forgot about the past and let the happier times prevail."

Happier times that would dissolve quickly.

"The day it got worse was when Henry tricked you into the maze. Elizabeth was inconsolable. You were everything to her."

George looks troubled, and some part of me stands taller to hear I was everything to a mother I barely remembered. "She lashed out at Henry, and in turn, your father. She brought up Sorcha and her belief that he had killed her. She knew Alex was being held here as a taunt for Asher to reappear. So, he had her locked away."

I scratch my neck and try to catch my breath with what he's telling me. "Alex was a captive?" That wasn't something I found easy to believe.

"Yes, but I watched over him. Henry had a fondness for Alex, so I knew he would never harm him. I kept Asher updated on what was happening."

"How could Asher have left his son like that?"

"You don't fear your father like the rest of us. He favors you, so you never see how deep he has embedded his darkness into the community. He has sculpted it into something we don't recognize or support anymore."

"We? As in you and Asher?"

"There are more of us that want change, and now I think we have a real opportunity to change things."

I sit back. "With me?" I question.

"If your father is removed, you will rise in his place. It's a far more powerful position than you can imagine. We needed to make sure you weren't like him. I tried over the years to nurture you without showing my hand. I tried to continue your mother's work, but most times it was impossible."

I think of all the things I had done for my father. All the beatings and punishments. I shift in my seat.

"I'm not going to lie to you, Lucas. I never supported the idea of you taking over. I really had believed we lost you to your father's ways."

I'm surprised at George's lack of belief in me. I try to hide the hurt his words are causing.

"But then I saw you with Ella and knew if we were going to strike, the time was now."

I didn't like the word *we*. Once again, I wanted to ask who, but really deep down, I wanted to ask if my mother was involved the whole time.

"Asher said that the person who killed his wife killed Declan."

George nods.

"So my father killed Declan?"

"Yes. He didn't exactly approve of that relationship." There's no sympathy in George's voice.

"What about the fingers?" I'm standing now, and I don't feel comfortable sitting down any longer. I glance at the hallway, thinking of Ella.

"I put them there. I removed both fingers. It was tradition and the only part that I could hold on to. I left them in Henry's possession because I honestly thought he would take them to your father and rattle him. But that didn't happen."

"I found them," I state while running my hands across my face.

"Thirty years, George?" I stop pacing. "That's a long time to conspire against him." *And do nothing but sit on your hands.*

"Thirty years since his first kill. We had some good years too, Lucas. But since he had your mother locked away, things have worsened and spiraled out of control. When I realized I wasn't alone, I came to Asher with the solution to his problem. If he helped us remove Andrew, he would have his son back."

George stands now too and pushes his hands into his pockets. "It's been a long road, but too many have died and suffered at your father's hands."

All his words are making me wonder what would have happened if I wasn't the right fit in their eyes.

"My father said he didn't kill Declan." A part of me cringes at my own words.

"He did, but I knew he would. It was only a matter of time before he took that from Henry. Your father has groomed Henry into a darker version of himself. Henry…" George dwindles off, and my stomach squeezes.

"Henry is lost to us. He will be a casualty in all this."

I'm staring at George. I'm not a fan of Henry, but I'm not going to throw him to the side. What Henry said about George hating him was starting to sound true.

"This is not his doing. Why should Alex be saved and not Henry?"

"Alex is aware of who he is and his reasoning for staying in that house. He gets us information that we would never gain otherwise. Henry trusts Alex."

"Once again, Henry is being betrayed," I shout, not for my love of Henry, but I don't know who to believe.

"Henry is dangerous, Lucas. You know that. He has killed as well."

"So have I," I shout again as it all rises to the surface. I don't have clean hands in all this. How many lives have I taken? How many beatings have resulted in deaths?

George steps up to me. "Yes, you have. But that was at your father's orders."

I shake my head.

"Henry enjoys it. You don't. There's a huge difference here."

My mind can't fully accept everything he's telling me.

"What do you want from me?"

"To be a leader. To use your power wisely."

"I still don't understand how you all just didn't remove my father already."

George looks sad and old. I hate how old he looks. "If we struck too soon, Lucas, and you took his place and became him, when would it stop? Would we have to remove you too?

We needed to make sure we made the right decision. Your mother wanted to make sure she made the right decision when she claims back her rights."

Blood pools into my feet. "Claims back her rights?"

"You're safe. You're out of your father's hands. Once you stay here, she has nothing to fear." George's eyes light up with possibilities.

"He locked her away once. What would stop him from doing it again?"

"Because she's not standing alone this time. We have two committee members on our side."

How deep does all this run? "Who?" I ask, but I think I already know.

"Aine and Sean. I know this is a lot to take in."

I half laugh, but there's no humor in it. The understatement of the year.

"There's so much more to tell you, but right now, you need to prepare yourself."

"For what?" What more could I be asked to prepare myself for?

"Your mother will be here soon."

My mother. I'm finally going to see my mother.

CHAPTER FOURTEEN

ELLA

I pace the floor as I wait for what feels like an eternity. Twice, I've raced for the door when I heard Lucas's voice rise, but both times it died down quickly. I want to know what's going on, but I also want to make sure he's safe.

Seeing Alex brought up so many emotions in me. He made me think of Hannah and Jessie, who I missed so much. I couldn't understand why he was taunting Lucas so much earlier, especially since he knows that Lucas is stronger than him.

I'm at the door again, and I want to open it. It moves and I step back as Lucas enters the room. He looks pale. His eyes are wide and filled with worry.

"What's wrong?"

He blinks and the worry gets buried amid the darkness.

"What's going on?" My anxiety is rising.

"My mother will be here soon."

Lucas sounds so young. There's a vulnerability on his face.

"What do you need me to do?" I would do anything for him. Even if that means staying in here. I would have a path worn in the floor, but right now I know he needed space.

"I want you with me."

Not what I expected, but I nod my head. "Whatever you need."

He closes the space between us and leans his forehead against mine. No words are spoken, and I wrap my arms around his waist as his breath fans out across my face. His eyes are closed, and I hate that I can't ease whatever turmoil is swirling inside him.

"You are going to hear things about me that aren't nice."

"What kind of things?" I whisper.

He doesn't shy away. "Bad things, Ella."

I swallow. The sad part is, I don't think anything could scare me away.

"Okay."

Lucas smiles, but it's filled with sadness. "No matter what, please remember I love you."

My heart bounces around in my chest. "I know. I love you too."

His kiss sears my lips and penetrates my heart.

"You keep me calm." I'm not sure if he's telling me or himself.

"That's you calm?" I ask, remembering him with Asher and Alex.

His brows draw down at my question, and he takes my face in his hands.

"You have no idea how much I want to hurt them."

My stomach twists and tightens. Lucas leans in and places his forehead against mine. He inhales deeply.

"Hurt them how?" I manage to squeak out my thoughts. Lucas releases me and steps back. Running a hand across his face, he looks unsure now.

"Like kill them?" I ask.

His head snaps up to me, and deep down in his eyes, I see something I've never seen before. Fear.

"No. Just hurt them." His answer is delivered slowly, and I'm picturing him beating a man so badly that his hands crack and split. My eyes flicker to his tight fists, and they move behind his back.

"Ella." There's a pleading in his eyes and voice.

I'm shaking my head. "No, I know that look. This is the part where you try to run from me."

His lips tug up. "I'm not running, and if I was..." He takes the few steps back to me and captures me in his arms. "I'd be running with you."

A knock on the bedroom door has my chest tightening. Is this it?

Lucas doesn't release me. "Yes?"

George appears at the door, and I detangle myself from Lucas.

"It's time." The famous last words ring through my mind. Lucas doesn't look at me but follows George out of the room. Taking a final breath, my stomach rises and dips as I follow them out to the living room.

The first thing I notice is how stunning she is. Lucas is very like his father in looks, but he has his mother's plump lips and high cheekbones.

Her blonde hair is swept back from her face. Blue eyes soak up Lucas, and I want to look away. It feels too private, too intimate. The clothing is a simple pants suit, but it's elegant on her tall frame.

"Lucas." His name is spoken with so much pain.

I glance up to find George watching me. He gives a nod and leaves the room. Strong fingers tighten around my hand, and I focus on Lucas as he leads me to the couch and sandwiches me beside him.

His mother still stands near the fireplace, and she looks away from Lucas when he doesn't speak. She runs her hands across her jacket before sitting down in an armchair. When she looks back up, her pain is controlled. It's still there, but it's not pouring out onto the floor.

"You must have so many questions." She swallows as she speaks. She stares at Lucas without blinking. His hand tightens on my fingers, and I don't look at him.

"Why haven't you come to see me before?"

It's like a bomb is dropped in the room. I hate the agony in his words, the anger. I hear so much wrapped up in the sentence. I want to leave the room. This was too private, but Lucas keeps an iron grip on my hand.

"I couldn't. Your father made sure of that. But I'm here now." Her words are controlled, and for the first time, she looks at me.

"You must be Ella." Her soft smile has me offering up one of my own. I'm not sure what to do.

"Yes. Nice to meet you." I have to clear my throat at the end. Lucas's grip on my hand loosens.

"I don't understand why you never tried to kill him," Lucas tells her.

My heart starts to pound, and my stomach shifts at his statement. I want to glance at him and ask him if he's serious, but I know he is.

"And become him?" His mother's brow furrows. "I thought about it a lot." She gives a heartfelt smile. "To hold my baby one more time." Sadness drowns her words out. "I thought about you every night." Her lips tug down, and I can't look at her pain. It's too much. It's too much to have pain like that and to have the cure right beside you; only you're too far gone to see it.

"Why didn't you claim your right to stop him before?" Lucas brushes over her pain with his anger.

It takes her a moment to put herself together. "How could I? He locked me away in a madhouse. It would have been kinder to kill me than keep me locked away from you."

Don't cry. Don't cry. My eyes are brimming with tears that I want to shed for both of them. But I remind myself I'm his calm. I tighten my hold on Lucas's hand and he shifts.

"What about Sean and Aine? They would have helped you." Once again, Lucas leans on anger.

His mother shakes her head while wiping a lone tear off her cheek. "They have only joined us recently. Things have gotten really bad in the last year, and they started to voice their disapproval for your father. If I had their backing, I would never have waited so long." She pauses for a beat.

"Can I hold you?" Her voice wobbles.

"No." Lucas's is like ice, and I bite the inside of my jaw.

His mother nods and wipes another falling tear away. "We need to act soon, Those poor girls are in the house."

My spine straightens, and blood pounds in my ears.

"They were all sent home. They are safe." Lucas says it abruptly and rises, releasing my hand. I have no idea what's going on.

"Is that all?"

She seems as confused as I do.

"No, Sean and Aine are arriving soon and we can discuss tactics."

"What do you want from me?" Lucas stays standing, and I have no idea if I should too.

"Could you please sit down?" She begs him, but he doesn't budge.

I say his name softly, and he looks at me for the first time. This must be so hard on him. I forget about the woman sitting across from us and smile just for Lucas.

He sits down slowly, and I take his large hand in mine. He keeps looking at me, and I let the world dissolve around us. I want to tell him it's okay, that his pain must be unbearable, but I'm here for him. I can't use my words, so I raise his hand to my mouth and place a kiss on it.

I want to tell him he's doing great, and I hope my eyes tell him all my lips can't say.

"All we need is for you to lead." His mother's words pierce our bubble, and I face her. She glances at me before looking back at her son.

"We will deal with him."

"How, when you clearly couldn't deal with him before?"

Lucas's mother flinches.

"Like I said, this time I have Sean and Aine, two committee members that will give me their vote."

"But father has two with Cathal and Bernard." Lucas's words are more clipped.

"Yes, but Asher is a witness to a murder Andrew committed. He would never count on Asher standing up to him, and now that Alex is out of there, Asher has nothing to fear."

Lucas exhales loudly. I peek at him. He looks tired. "What about Henry?"

His mother's face freezes, her light blue eyes darkening. "You know your father allowed him to visit me?"

Lucas's fingers tighten around mine.

"Why not me?" My heart squeezes again. They come out as an accusation, but I hear his pain at the end of each word.

His mother's lips tug down, and she's fighting not to cry. She swallows. "Because you're all I wanted. He took away the best part of me." Her tears spill but she holds still, staring at Lucas. Staring at her baby.

Her pain has me looking away again.

"Henry... is so like Andrew," she continues. "He got the worst part of your father. He's cruel and likes hurting people.

He used to tease me, tell me stories about you. I would hang onto his last word, and then he would confess to making it all up."

Lucas is like stone beside me, and I glance at him to see if he's even breathing.

He needs to let go of the pain he's holding on to. Their pain is choking me. He asked me to stay, but I think he needs me to leave.

"I'm going to get some fresh air. Is that okay?" I ask him. His head snaps to me, and as painful as it is, I know I'm making the right decision. His eyes are far away, but slowly, he comes back to me.

"Don't go far."

I smile up into his handsome face. "I won't." I kiss his lips softly. "I love you."

His frame relaxes. "I love you, too."

I don't want to leave him, but he needs this time with his mother. No words are spoken as I get up and leave the living room. I go out the back door, and the minute I step out onto the porch, I feel like I'm breathing for the first time. Their loss could never be removed, but seeing both of them in such pain made me hope they could at least find solace in each other eventually.

"A penny for your thoughts." I glance down at Alex as he walks toward the back steps, his hands behind his back. I hadn't noticed him when I stepped out onto the porch.

"You don't want to know my thoughts," I tell him. If he could see the mess inside my head right now, I don't think he would be asking me to share.

"What do you call a bear without any teeth?" Alex steps up on the bottom step. I want to tell him I'm not in the mood for his jokes, but it will take my mind off what's happening behind me.

"I don't know," I answer.

He smiles at me.

"Come on, Ella. Try."

I exhale loudly and try to think. "A bear with no teeth?"

His laughter is musical, and I remember why I liked him. He had a nice way about him. He clears the last step. "A gummy bear."

I snort a laugh. "You need to get better material."

He walks behind me. "Are you not entertained?" He steps up beside me.

"Maybe a little," I confess.

He laughs again. "That smile tells me it's more than a little."

Silence falls between us as we both stare out onto the white world.

"I miss it."

I glance at Alex.

"I miss the house; I miss Henry. " His confession has him shrugging before stuffing his hands into his jeans pockets. "I had hated it at first, but it kind of grew on me. It's all I have ever known."

"I'm sorry, Alex." How many people had Andrew damaged? The list was growing and growing.

He shrugs again and smiles sadly.

"How bad is it in there?" He indicates with his chin to the house.

"It's really sad that they were kept apart." I grip the railing.

"I'd say you regret the first day you stepped foot into the house. You didn't think you would end up here."

"I never thought for one second that the road would be this hard," I admit. "But I don't regret a thing."

I glance back at the house as if I can see through the wall and see Lucas.

"I found Lucas." I smile and allow my love to show.

Alex doesn't seem happy at all. He frowns. "I don't get that." His words are delivered with a sharp head shake.

"I'm not asking you to." I speak to the trees. I don't need anyone else judging us.

"You're so nice."

I glance at him. "So is he," I defend.

Alex shakes his head. "Maybe to you, Ella, but not the rest of us."

Asher appears around the back, and I'm so glad to see him. Being alone with Alex feels stifling now.

"I see everyone has escaped the house." He smiles up at Alex, and I can't believe how I didn't make the connection the moment I saw him. Alex has his father's dancing eyes. He looks like he's filling up with mischief, and no matter what, I just want to be involved.

"I thought some fresh air would be nice." I fold my arms across my chest. I feel like I'm standing with Lucas's enemies. They really aren't, but he sees them as that.

"Get plenty now, because Sean and Aine will be here soon, and it's best if we're all together."

I nod. *Oh God, a room with us all together.*

"We will need you, Ella."

I know I'm going to be there for Lucas, but the way Asher is looking at me is different.

"I'll be there with Lucas," I say.

"Not for Lucas, but as you. You do understand when he takes his place as our leader, so will you."

My stomach somersaults.

"He's picked you to marry, so you will hold fifty percent power."

I feel silly standing here like he's talking rubbish, but his words make sense. I just never thought about what came with marrying Lucas. I just dreamed of falling in love. I was so naïve.

"Thousands of lives will depend on you."

No pressure.

I nod.

"I know nothing is official yet, but Aine and Sean are meeting you as a new leader too. So first impressions are everything."

I'm aware of the sneakers on my feet and, no doubt, my disheveled look.

"She understands." Alex speaks up for me, and I glance at him. His words are clipped, and it's not something I've heard from him before.

I don't need him speaking on my behalf.

"I'll do my best," I tell Asher. I hope I sound strong, because inside, I feel frightened and lost.

I'm not ready to rule.

CHAPTER FIFTEEN

LUCAS

My mother keeps reaching for me, and I don't want her to touch me. I don't recognize her. She looks older, like a copy of the woman I remember. She's watching me like I might vanish. I can't allow her pain to register with me. She wants us to hug and to cry it out, but I still don't understand why she didn't just kill him.

"You left us in his hands," I say and tighten my fists. It wasn't just me. Henry was left too.

"He locked me up."

"So you keep repeating." I'm angry at her. I'm angry at him. I don't want excuses.

"Because I couldn't leave. I was locked up and watched twenty-four hours a day. If they weren't shoving tablets down my throat, they had Henry torment me." She stands now, her words oozing from her. I see the cracks. I see the damage.

"All I want is my baby back." Her eyes blur as she stares at me.

I'm staring at her, and I don't recognize this woman. I don't feel a memory tug at me. Her smell isn't taking me back to my stolen childhood.

I focus on the here and now. "So how did you escape?"

She flinches at my words, but it pulls her out of her own despair and makes her think. "I learned the more I fought, the worse it got.

So, I obeyed them. They stopped drugging me and I stopped asking for you." Her lips drag down again.

"They slowly started to trust me. The first time I escaped, I made it to the house." She smiles through her pain. "I managed to make it all the way to your bedroom door before he caught me." She blinks and tears fall.

She wipes her face and turns her back on me.

"You shouldn't have returned. He would have expected that." My words aren't fair.

"I know. It took me years to learn that."

I tighten my jaw and glance out the large window. I don't see Ella, but I can hear voices chirping on the porch. I wonder who she's talking to.

"She's lovely."

I turn to my mother. She's sitting again and seems more composed. I nod, not wanting to talk about Ella.

"The way she looks at you—"

"I don't want to talk about Ella. Let's just focus on what we need to do." I'm not trying to be cruel, but I don't know her.

Her blue eyes spark with a touch of anger, but she nods. I raise my hands, itchy with a need to touch Ella.

I turn my back on my mother and my stomach twists. I always thought when I finally got to see her I would be overjoyed. But right now, all I want to do is hurt someone, hurt her, so I walk away.

Opening the back door, my anger escalates. Ella stares at me and so does Alex, who stands too fucking close to her. I step out onto the porch and pull the door behind me. It's hard to let go of the handle. I release Ella from my stare and glance at Asher, who stands in the snow. What were they all talking about?

I step up to Ella. Pitching Alex over the rail seems like something that would release a tiny bit of my anger. He's tracking me. I wonder if he can see his doom played out in my eyes. I take Ella's hand in mine, and her head snaps up. Relief swims in her eyes, and I raise her hand to my mouth and kiss it, just like she did for me. I want to thank her for being here.

"Aine and Sean are arriving any minute." Asher's words aren't harsh. I expected them to be.

I wanted to say *my mother*, but meeting her makes me understand that she's a stranger to me.

Asher's brows rise, and I want him to say something. Give me a reason to lash out.

"Why don't we take a walk?" Ella's words surprise me, and a walk sounds like something I could do right now. To have her alone has my shoulders relaxing.

"I don't think that's wise." Asher speaks to Ella, and I'm ready to tell him to mind his fucking business.

"We won't be long, Asher. Just a short walk." Ella tactfully speaks while stepping off the porch. She holds my hand tightly as we walk past Asher. He doesn't look happy, but he wisely keeps his mouth shut.

"Have you ever seen a wishing well?"

I smile at Ella as she speaks. "No, have you?" I'm sure she has.

She shakes her head. "No."

Her eyes are light as she smiles up at me. "Well, in *Snow White*, there is a wishing well."

I laugh. I should have known we would be going back to her fairy tales.

"Don't laugh. This is serious stuff."

I want to kiss her, with her flushed cheeks and red lips. She looks beautiful, but I don't stop her as she continues to walk towards the trees.

"In one of the scenes, *Snow White* sings into the wishing well, and it echoes back at her. It was like her wish was confirmed once she heard it back. It stuck with me."

We step into the tree line. "So we're searching for a wishing well?"

She smiles and with each step I take with her, I shed my anger. She makes me feel light.

"No, we aren't looking for a wishing well." She stops and looks around her. "This will be fine." She releases my hand and stands directly in front of me so we're facing each other.

"I am your wishing well." She takes a bow.

I grin. "I can wish for anything?"

She nods and I've never seen Ella look so excited. "Once I echo it back, it means it will come true."

I crack my knuckles and rotate my neck, and Ella laughs. "Here goes. I wish for Ella to be in my arms and pressing her lips against mine."

Her laugh is quick, and her cheeks flush more. "As nice as that sounds, I won't echo it. So it's not coming true."

She steps up to me. "Close your eyes."

I do.

"I want you to really think about what you would wish for."

I keep my eyes closed but can hear her step away.

"I wish I could keep Ella forever." My stomach twists.

"I wish I could keep Ella forever." Her words are so soft that I open my eyes and look at her. A part of me doesn't want to do this.

"Keep going." She encourages me.

For her, I do. "I wish this would all end."

She smiles sadly. "I wish this would all end."

"I wish…"

I exhale loudly. I don't want to do this. Ella's wide green eyes stare at me, so I continue.

"I wish I didn't feel so angry."

Ella nods. "I wish I didn't feel so angry," she echoes.

"You have such a beautiful mind." I take a step to Ella. "If all the wishes I made would really come true, then I wish for one more."

Ella nods. "Don't wish for me to be naked in the snow or something like that."

I laugh. "Don't tempt me."

"I wish Ella O'Leary never changes, no matter what."

Her smile is mesmerizing. Squatting down, I brush aside snow and root out a small stone. After picking it up, I close the distance between me and Ella.

"I wish Ella O'Leary never changes, no matter what." Ella's voice is low. She's focused on my hand, and I open it. "Remember this place."

Her smile wobbles as she takes the stone from my hand. Her eyes water as they focus on me. "I could never forget it."

"I could never forget you, Lucas." Something beyond my understanding burns in her eyes as she reaches up and touches my face. Pain leaks from her eyes.

"She didn't forget you either."

My heart pounds, and I fight with everything inside me.

I want to look away as Ella bends and shifts.

"She's hurting as much as you."

The last time I cried was when my dog died. I feel so beat down. A tear slips, and Ella looks ready to fall apart. I pull her into my arms. She's my anchor. I reel it all back in and focus on my love for her.

She's the ground under my feet. The wall at my back. She's what makes my heart beat. She's my strength and my weakness. She's my everything.

CHAPTER SIXTEEN

ELLA

I'm choking. I can't breathe. He's clinging to me, and I'm telling myself not to think. My hands claw and pull at his back, bringing him closer to me. I want to take it all away.

He's not crying, but he's breaking, and I wish he would let it out but he won't. It's forcing its way out of him in the most painful way.

"Ella." Alex's voice is like a gunshot. Lucas lets me go but doesn't turn to Alex.

I step out of Lucas's arms.

"Everyone is waiting." Alex's face is tense. His eyes flicker to Lucas's heaving back.

"We will be there in a minute." I keep my chin held high.

His eyes flicker again at Lucas, and I feel protective.

"I said we will be there in a minute." My tone cuts Alex's attention back to me before he leaves. I watch him the whole way back to the house before I turn back to Lucas. I'm drowning, and I know I need to swim.

I hate how his hands hang at his sides like he's defeated. When he glances at me, I can't stop the smile that spreads across my face. His eyes haven't given up. A war rages in them, and I know today we might have won the battle, but we still have to face the war. I'm okay with that.

I reach out my hand and he takes it. I have Lucas, and right now that's all that matters. The world could fall at our feet, but I know once I have him, I'm fine.

"Are you ready?" I ask.

"No." His answer is said with a heavy shake of his head.

I'm smiling at him again. He must think I'm crazy, but he's fighting. Whether he's ready or not, he's fighting.

We walk back to the house, and I want to say something he can hold on to or something that people say.

"Break a leg" pops out of my mouth as we step up on the porch.

"You want me to break their legs?"

The darkness that swirls in his eyes tugs his lips up into a grin.

I lean in and press my lips against his. "No. Don't break their legs," I say as I lean out.

He's smiling, and I don't want him to ever take it off. "If I do, it's because you said so." His serious tone doesn't match his teasing eyes as he pulls the back door open.

"I didn't. I said for you to break your leg," I say while following him in.

"Such violence." He tuts, and I can't stop the smile that's eating away my sadness.

The noise in the living room is loud as we enter. I rub my hands on my jeans as I follow Lucas into the kitchen area, where everyone is seated. The noise ceases as we enter. A woman, who is seated to the left of Lucas's mother, holds the room. She's watching me, and when our eyes meet, her thin lips raise in a slight smile.

"Ella O'Leary, we finally get to meet you." Her eyes are wide, with fake thick black lashes surrounding them. She stands, holding out both hands.

I want to look at Lucas, but I don't. I take the lady's outstretched hands. She covers my hand with both of hers. She smells like someone who spent the last few hours at a spa, a mixture of oils, perfumes, and creams emitting from her.

"I'm Aine, one of the committee members." Her eyes hold steady. She's commanding and can hold her own.

"Lovely to meet you, Aine."

She releases my hand and sits down. Lucas's mother watches me.

Lucas holds out a seat for me at the other end of the table, and I sit down.

"We should start with a brief introduction of who we are for Ella."

Ugh, this is like the first day of school. Not that I went to school, but I saw it on TV. The new girl either became the thing of interest or the target. I'm not sure which I would prefer.

Once Lucas sits beside me, Aine takes the floor, establishing herself. "I have been a member for over thirty years. My father sat on the committee with Master Andrew's father."

"I don't think we should refer to him as Master Andrew." A man with a gray mustache speaks up.

Aine isn't put out by the correction. She smiles at the man. "Of course, Lucas's father." She raises a brow, and when the man sits back, she passes it over to Lucas's mother.

"We've already met."

"I'm Sean, a committee member along with Aine, and we want change. You're young but we were young once too, and with our guidance, I think we can change our community and restore it to what it once was."

"Nice to meet you, Sean." Since the introductions were spoken to me, I felt the need to respond, no matter how uncomfortable I felt.

Lucas touches my bouncing leg. I hadn't noticed I was rocking it under the table. I stop as his touch relaxes me.

Next at the table is Asher, with Alex sitting beside him. Alex's blue eyes are ice as he stares at me, and I have no idea what I've done to receive such hostility. Lucas is at the head of the table, his mother at the other end. Beside me is George.

I count eight of us. Eight people with one objective: to remove Andrew from power.

"Now that we all know each other, I would like you to explain why you ran, Lucas." Aine speaks carefully, and she still wears that smile on her thin lips, but there's something far more calculating in her eyes.

"I'm pretty sure you know why, Aine." Lucas sounds hostile already, and I lower my hand under the table and slowly touch his hand that still rests on my knee. I don't look at him, but I hope he relaxes a bit.

"I understand that Ella was being punished, but to run isn't a sign of a very good leader."

"I thought you came here to help us." Lucas's mother defends him as she faces Aine.

I cringe at the table.

"I did, Elizabeth. You know how dangerous this is. But I would like to think I can place my trust in Lucas. Again." She turns to Lucas, and I feel I should say something.

"Once my father is removed, I will never have a reason to leave again." Lucas's words are ground out through his teeth.

"I think we can all agree that we need to move past Lucas's leaving and focus on what's important." Sean speaks up, looking up and down the table. Aine turns her head away, but not before I catch her eye.

She resents me. I see it in her eyes. I took their upcoming leader away. Can I blame her? I have no idea what I'm getting myself into. Once again, I feel so out of my depth. I'm looking for love, not to become a leader and have people lean on me.

"Since you left, Master Lucas, Andrew has abused his power even further. Matthew Crowley has stepped in as a committee member, backing up every reckless decision your father makes." Sean's eyes are tight around the edges.

"My son was due to marry, just like you. But your father has changed everything. There's no longer a selection process."

"That's not a bad thing, Sean." Lucas speaks up and everyone falls silent.

"It's tradition, Master Lucas." Sean is different from Aine. His eyes hold fear that hers don't. Even the way he addresses Lucas is different.

"We'll make new ones, better ones. I don't think the selection process is fair to the six girls who aren't selected." Lucas glances at me, and I tighten my hold on his hand.

Sean nods.

"I think that is the least of our worries. We need to focus on the problem at hand." Aine speaks directly to Sean, who sits further back in his chair.

"Asher is a witness to Andrew murdering Sorcha." Elizabeth swallows. "He has offered to come forward and make a statement."

All eyes land on Asher, who nods his head in agreement.

"He killed my wife." His eyes touch everyone, and I think of the clothes upstairs, all the boxes.

I want to tell Asher I'm sorry. I hope he can see it in my eyes when he looks at me. He seems softer now.

"Andrew has been searching for me for a long time," Asher says.

Aine nods. "Yes, I'm aware of a bounty on Asher Bradley's head. Your crime was never stated, which is interesting now, because of what you witnessed."

Aine still wears that smile, and I don't know if it's too much Botox that has her lips set into a permanent smile or if she's just that self-assured.

"Ella's branding is in three days." Lucas's mother speaks up.

Lucas nearly crushes my fingers in his hand. My stomach plummets. "He's still going ahead with the gathering?" He sounds shocked.

"We're counting on it. It's there we will make our appearance and publicly call him out on his crimes. Can you imagine how many other people he has hurt?" Lucas's mother speaks directly to him.

"Can you imagine how many other people he made wealthy and gave power to?" Lucas fires back before he looks to Aine. "This is the best plan you could all come up with?"

"We're being smart, Lucas. There's no point in us trying to force him out with just us. The people hate him too. If we're in front of them when we present the truth, they'll see, and on that stage, we can cast a vote." Aine sounds very sure.

"When your father left, he gave you the power to punish Declan's murder." George speaks up.

I have no idea what's going on, but all I'm hearing is people being murdered. I try to keep still like I know all this.

George's voice rings across the room. "That still stands. He transferred that power to you, for that task." George smiles. "We know who killed Declan."

"Can you prove it?" Lucas asks.

"Henry confessed to me," Alex says.

I try not to move on. I don't want to miss a beat. I have no idea what's going on and a part of me is angry that Lucas allowed me to step into this meeting so blind.

"Henry knew?" Lucas sounds shocked again.

"Henry is another matter that needs to be addressed." Aine speaks up at the end of the table, and Sean and Elizabeth bob their heads in agreement.

"He said his father was jealous of his love for Declan, so he understood it. He has a different way of seeing things." Alex frowns, and I think of his confession outside about missing Henry. It makes me question the type of person that he is.

"He did lock me in a refrigerator then, saying he was protecting me." Alex frowns as he stares at the table.

"So both Bradleys are our witnesses to take down my father and Henry?" Lucas says and a lull falls around the table. "My father had an affair with their mother. Henry was the result. So how does this look? Like one angry family going up against the other."

For the first time, I feel not as lost with this meeting. I knew about Henry and the affair.

"It's the truth," Asher says. His eyes focus on Lucas. "That's all that matters at the end, Lucas. The truth. When we stop lying, only then can we rebuild." Asher's eyes are heavy with time lost.

"I agree." Aine speaks up.

"Me too." Sean is next, and there are nods going around the table until it stops at Lucas.

"Where do Ella and I come into this?" Lucas glances at me before turning back to everyone. I hate how everyone watches me now.

"You both will be there," Aine says.

Lucas starts shaking his head. "Ella will not be present. She will stay here."

I want to protest because I'm not staying here without him.

"She will lead as much as you. We need both of you to make a stand against Andrew. He's claiming that Ella is to be branded and that

Sandra is your wife. He's still sticking to these claims, so when you arrive with Ella as your bride-to-be, it will prove how much he lies."

Aine has a point, and I completely agree with her. I don't know what shift I've made, but her eyes land on me. "Don't you agree?"

My heart pounds in my chest. "I think me hiding will only serve Andrew's agenda." I look to Lucas. "I'll be safer with you."

My heart bounces in my chest as he holds my stare. I see the war in his eyes, while mine are pleading. His lashes close, cutting me off before he faces the table.

"Ella will be with us." He doesn't sound happy.

Aine is still watching me, but there's something different in her eyes now.

"The gathering is in three days, so we will strike then." Lucas's mother speaks up, and it's the first time I've heard her sounding nervous. Everyone gives their agreement to this arrangement.

"Who's hungry?" Asher asks.

"Starving." Aine's smile stretches a little bit more, making her eyes look wider. She catches me looking at her, and I look away.

Lucas finally lets my hand go. "Are you okay?" His words are low and just for me, but Alex sits across from us, watching me. I want to ask him what his problem is.

"Yes."

Aine steps up beside Lucas. "Could I have a word in private?"

"I won't be long." Lucas tells me, and I wave him off as he leaves the room with Aine.

No one is at the table, only me and Alex, and I don't want to be alone with him.

"I'm glad I finally got you alone." My heart leaps as Lucas's mother touches my shoulder and sits down in the chair that Lucas just vacated.

She's holding a steaming cup of coffee. I wonder if that is why Lucas likes coffee.

"He won't speak to me." Her words are soft.

"I'm sorry."

She shrugs my apology away. "It's not your fault. I see how responsive he is to you. I was wondering if you could talk to him."

I shift. This is uncomfortable and even more so with Alex staring at me. "I... I think he just needs some time. It's a lot to take in."

She nods. "But you will try?"

"Yes, I will." She rises at my response and touches my shoulder again.

I glance out into the living area for Lucas, but he isn't there. I don't want to stay in here any longer. Everyone is making me uncomfortable. I decide I'm not the new thing or the target. I'm a tool that they'll use against Lucas.

CHAPTER SEVENTEEN

LUCAS

A ine insists on privacy, so I take her to my room. Closing the door, she folds her arms in front of herself.

"Are you sure of your choice?" She isn't judging. Aine is coming from a place of knowledge. I know her words don't have a double meaning or a hidden one. It still irritates me to be questioned, but I also need to remember she'll be making up the next committee.

"Yes."

She nods and accepts my response. "I don't want to bring this up at the table with Ella present, but the girls aren't doing so good, Lucas. I don't know how much more time they have."

I run my hands across my face. I know they're being kept there, but to think of anything happening to them has my stomach twisting. Ella would be devastated if either of them was hurt.

"What's happened to them?" I need to know if we can save them or if we're better off letting them go.

"I'm not entirely sure, but they've been left in Henry's hands. Mark was the one who came to me. He told me if I had a way to reach you, then now would be the time."

Mark is my father's servant. What would prompt him to reach out to Aine? What is Henry doing to those girls?

"Henry has rooms under the shed. That's where they're being held." Aine looks uncomfortable, and I don't blame her.

"Both of them are being judged at the gathering for conspiring against Henry."

I shake my head. My father is showing his true self. "If they are, then they will be alive." That has to count for something.

"*Should be* alive, Lucas. I just wanted to inform you so you can tell Ella in a gentler way."

"I won't be telling her. None of you will." I drive each word home so Aine hears me.

"I don't think that's wise."

I want to reach out and grab Aine around her throat. "I don't care if you think it's wise or not. I said she will not be told."

Aine bristles but nods her head. "Your word is final."

"Yes, it is," I state, hoping to drive home my point.

We'll save Hannah and Jessie at the gathering. But Ella having that knowledge now would torment her. I'll deal with her anger later. She doesn't need to suffer unnecessarily.

"I also want to talk about the matter of Henry."

I don't want to talk anymore. The thought of Ella finding out about Hannah and Jessie has my stomach quivering. I can't let that happen. It will kill her to know they're being hurt.

"He needs to be fully removed."

"I will think about it."

Aine isn't satisfied. "I left that book for you, Lucas. So you would understand the power you could wield."

That surprises me. I thought it was George. "You want me to hang Henry because he's gay?"

Aine shrugs. "You have a reason and the power. Why not?"

"No." I'm not going to do it. We have to come up with a more fitting punishment.

"If you let him live, he will forever be a torment."

"When we deal with my father, everyone will have a fair vote on what to do with Henry."

That seems to satisfy Aine.

"Is that everything?" I want to leave this room.

"Yes."

We return to the kitchen area, and my eyes scan the room, but Ella isn't present and neither is Alex. I tighten my fists.

"I wanted to see if you could listen to my ideas about the new structure."

I'm glaring out the window, trying to see if I can see Ella.

"I think that would be interesting," Aine says.

I look at Sean. "Of course." I don't want to, but that's what came with this job. A lot of things I don't want to do.

Asher brings sandwiches and teas to the table as everyone sits down. No one mentions Alex's and Ella's whereabouts. Asher pours everyone tea except me.

"Would you like a coffee?" My mother is watching me from the end of the table.

"No." I look away from her prodding eyes.

The chairs on either side of me are empty, and it has me tightening my fists. I want to look for her, but I know I need to give her space, too. Not having her beside me feels wrong.

"I like our structure. I think some traditions should be kept and some reinstated. So, for example: We had a yearly gathering for all the people to meet each other. I think we should bring that back."

I don't care, but I sit up knowing I need to look like I do. "We can cast a vote once we have a stable setting."

"I think we can discuss what happens to Henry now." Aine slides it in like I didn't just tell her we would vote on it after dealing with my father.

She looks up at me, and I need her on my side. But she must also know my power. "Aine is right."

She smiles.

"We will have to vote on it, but not until my father has been removed."

"I think that is wise," Sean says.

"Sean, if you feel a structure you have will work, present it on the first meeting of our new committee. We will vote and implement it then."

"I want to ask about my son," Sean says.

I try not to show my frustration.

"He wants the girls that were presented brought back and for the process to continue."

I don't want that to happen.

"Don't you think it's the least of our worries?" Aine sings, and I allow it.

"I know any son of yours is a good person, Sean. But with all that has transpired, I don't think any ladies should be placed in any houses until we can come up with something more effective. There are too many who abuse their power." I look at each person at the table. "It has to stop."

Sean nods his head, but he isn't exactly overjoyed.

"Now, excuse me." I stand. The itch to find Ella is overwhelming. I reach the living room, when my mother stops me.

"Lucas, can I just have a moment?" I know the other members are watching, and I can't show disrespect.

I turn to her, but I can't find words. She makes my blood boil. "Yes."

"Please, just give me a chance."

"I am," I say and glance out the window. The snow is falling again. She touches my hand, and I pull away. "Don't touch me."

She's holding me to her chest as she runs. Her smell surrounds me, and she scream fosr help. Her heart beat is so fast against my ear. I'm surrounded by her, and I know I'm safe.

The memory dwindles, and I step back from her. The smell of her perfume was a trigger. She's still standing too close, causing memories to rise in me. Memories I don't want to deal with right now.

"You are my son." She tightens her fists at her side, and I can't stop the vicious smirk that takes over my face.

"If you had kept your hands off Henry, maybe you wouldn't have lost me. Because of your actions, I ended up being raised by him. You think it was easy?" I take a step toward her. "You think you had it tough behind your locked door?" I sneer. "You have no idea what I endured. What I have done."

"My only downfall was loving you too much." She shakes her head, and I hate looking into her watery eyes. "I just want a second chance with my baby."

"I don't think I can give you what you want." I growl my frustration. Her shoulders fall in defeat. "I'm not the boy you left behind. I'm sorry, but he's gone."

And I'm in his place. I can remember her, but I can't connect the dots enough to feel the safety she once offered me. She was laughter and bedtime stories to that little boy that adored his mother. But that isn't me.

"Let me try, Lucas." She reaches for me again, and her hand falls to her side as I step away.

"Just do your job on the committee. Leave me out of it." I walk away and to the window. The snow is still falling, and close to the tree line I see a figure in black. My heart jumps. It's Ella and she isn't alone. Beside her is Alex. They both have their backs to me.

But they lean into each other like they're talking.

CHAPTER EIGHTEEN

ELLA

The snow falls in a steady stream around us. I can't look at Alex.

"You want to tell me what we are doing out here in the freezing cold?"

My heart beats wildly. My mind is skipping over Aine's words to Lucas's response. Hannah and Jessie are in Henry's grasp. They never left that house. Pain radiates through me. What happened to them? I had left them! My chest tightens and I rub it.

"Do you remember seeing Hannah and Jessie in the house?"

I need it confirmed. I need to know if Lucas lied to me. I found Alex after I had crept away from the door and dragged him out here.

The branches of the trees bend with the weight of the snow.

"Yes, your friends. What is this about Ella?" Alex faces me.

"Just focus on the tree line. I don't want it to look like we're talking," I say.

"So we look like we're standing in the snow staring at the trees?" I hate the humor in Alex's voice.

"Just answer my questions. Were all the girls sent home?"

Alex faces forward. "Yes, except for Hannah and Jessie."

A sob tears from me. "Do you know where they are?"

Alex doesn't answer me, and I look at him.

"Ella..." He's shaking his head. "What are you going to do?"

"Please, just tell me."

His eyes are conflicted, and I step up to him and grip his arm. "Please, Alex."

He looks at my hand on his. "Henry is keeping them in a cell under the shed."

My stomach turns and bile rises up my throat.

"Ella, you can't do anything."

I release Alex as the world spins. In the distance, I see Lucas making his way to us. My heart jumps. He told Aine I was not to be told.

How could he?

"Please don't mention this conversation." I glance at Alex. "Please, Alex."

He nods his head with furrowed brows.

"Are you trying to make yourself sick?" Lucas asks once he reaches us. Alex spins around.

I want to slap Lucas. My heart jumps as his dark eyes pin me in place.

"I just needed some air." My heart palpitates.

Lucas's eyes tighten, and he glares at Alex. "Did you do something to her?"

Alex pales and I laugh. Both of them look at me like I've lost my mind, and it feels a bit like that.

"You did. How stupid did I look in there?" I have no idea what's going on. "You let me step into that room blind." I'm shouting at him, when all I want to do is scream about how cruel he is for leaving Hannah and Jessie in Henry's hands.

"I didn't want to frighten you." His words are controlled.

"No, just make me look weak and stupid." I want to scream at him so badly.

"You didn't look weak or stupid. You did great." Lucas is looking at me like my outburst is unwarranted.

"I had no idea about people being murdered and Henry being involved." My heart breaks. I want him to tell me so we can do this together.

He's staring at me like I've lost my mind.

"Is there anything else you haven't told me? Because right now would be a good time."

I'm waiting and watching as snow lands on his dark hair and melts. He's a picture standing in the snow, and I hate him for that. I want him to fix this. I want him to go and get them and bring them here so they're safe.

I'm aware of how stiff Alex is beside me, but I can't contain the rage bubbling throughout my system.

"No. Now you know everything. I'm sorry I didn't tell you sooner," Lucas says.

Liar.

I want to call him out on it, but right now, I need distance from him before I say something I regret.

I shake my head and step away from him. He reaches out and grabs my wrist.

"Ella, is there something else bothering you? You know you can talk to me about anything."

I look up into dark eyes that flicker to Alex. He still thinks Alex said or did something to cause my anger. "No, Lucas. This is all on your shoulders. You kept me in the dark, and I don't appreciate it."

"I'm sorry. Tell me how I can fix this." His eyes plead with me, and I have a moment of just wanting to step into his arms and allow him to take it all away.

"I need space."

He flinches like I've slapped him. His fingers slip from my wrist, and the loss of contact is immediate.

I swallow as I walk away from Lucas. The snow is growing deeper, so I have to lift my legs higher. It's not the most graceful exit as I enter the house. Everyone is in the living space. Elizabeth looks at me with a smile, and I force one back. I dodge George's questioning look and Aine's smiling face as I enter my room and close the door.

I can't breathe as my lungs contract painfully. I need to calm down. Sitting on the edge of the bed, I place my head between my legs and take deep breaths in through my nose and out through my mouth. My heart won't slow, and I get that horrible feeling like it's not beating correctly. It feels like it's missing a beat.

Standing, I bounce on my feet, trying to help the blood rush throughout my body. The door opens and Lucas stands in the doorway. His hair is damp from the snow, and he runs his hands through it before closing the door behind him. My heart beats faster, and I turn away from him but continue to bounce on my feet.

"Not now, Lucas." I can't deal with him.

"I know you asked for space, but we need to talk about this."

Any other time, I would have loved to hear those words. Any other time, he would have disappeared, leaving me looking for him. But right now, I need to calm down.

"Why are you bouncing?" He moves around me, and I don't look up at him.

"I think I'm having a panic attack." Or a heart attack. My heart beat is off.

Lucas starts to bounce in front of me, mimicking my movements.

"What are you doing?" I finally look at him. My stomach twists.

"Helping you."

"By bouncing?" I exhale loudly before I inhale through my nose. Lucas copies me, and I want him to stop.

"You're not helping!" I bark and I swear I see humor in his dark eyes.

"I think I am. There's color in your cheeks." My heart beats fast, but it's not skipping beats. He wasn't helping me; he was distracting me. *Which, in turn, is helping*, a voice says in the back of my head.

"That's my temper," I say as I flex my hands. My heart rate is slowing.

"I know. Did I ever tell you how sexy you are when you're angry?" His smile is killing me.

Why did he have to lie to me? I hate him for making me feel bad, like I'm the one hurting him.

"I wish you would tell me the truth," I say and stop bouncing. So does he.

In the silence of the room, he has the perfect opportunity.

"I wish you would tell me the truth," he echoes.

"I am," I say and swallow. I'm not, but that's because he hasn't been.

"I never lied to you, Ella. I withheld information that I thought would be too heavy for you. I really thought all of this would get resolved quicker and you would never need to see the uglier part of my family."

He's right about the murders. I could have lived without knowing about them.

"But I need to know things that will affect me."

Lucas closes the distance and takes my face in his hands. "How do you feel now?"

"Better," I answer honestly. In his hands, I feel like we're the only two that exist. "Is there anything else you need to tell me, Lucas?"

His eyes search my face, and my heart starts to gallop. *Tell me and I will forgive you*, I plead with my eyes.

"No, I think you know everything now." He places his lips on my forehead. "I was only trying to protect you."

The kiss sears me, and I want to push him away. It's so easy to get lost with Lucas. It's like dreaming and then waking up. I need to wake up. I need to help Jessie and Hannah.

I lean into him and wrap my arms around his waist. His relief at my submission has him pulling me tighter to his chest while placing several kisses to the crown of my head.

"Asher is making dinner now. We better join the others." Lucas's voice rumbles through his chest, and I bite back the tears that want to spill.

"Let me freshen up, and I'll be there in a minute." I release Lucas and don't look at him as I step away. I need to let him believe that everything is fine.

"Are you okay now?" he asks.

I turn to him and force a smile. "An early night after dinner, and I'll be fine."

His eyes search my face, so I turn away and gather a clean jumper and trousers. I give one final smile before I make my way to the bathroom, where I wash my face and change my clothes. Tonight, when he sleeps, I'll leave and get Hannah and Jessie. I can't leave them down there. I know he'll be mad at me, but he'll forgive me. I'm willing to forgive him for not telling me.

I just need to get through these next few hours.

CHAPTER NINTEEN

LUCAS

I try to keep it together as I leave the bedroom. I'm going to kill him. She's lying to me, and I have no idea why she's hiding something from me. The only thing I can think of is Alex. What did he say to her outside? He looked so happy when she was shouting at me. The louder she got, the happier he was.

I tighten my fists and tell myself to remain somewhat calm. He's standing at the fireplace, talking to his father and Aine. The little fucker is smiling. His eyes flicker to me, and I still see that smile. He did something. I know it.

My mother watches me as I step into the space. She's ready to approach me, so I step away before she can corner me. After pulling off my damp jumper, I leave it on the back of a chair in the kitchen. I fix the black shirt I'm wearing under it as George arrives with a bowl of carrots and places them on the table.

He pauses. "I'm proud of you." They aren't words I've heard before. I stand straighter and look down at the old man. I see the pride in his eyes.

"You grew into a fine man, and you will make a great leader."

He has no idea the effect his words have on me. "Thank you, George."

He reaches up and grips my shoulder.

"Ella, I was telling Aine about my skills in jokes. You can testify to my greatness."

I freeze at Alex's voice. I try not to look over my shoulder.

"He's so bad. They fall flat." Ella's words are said with a fondness, and Aine laughs.

George's hand slips from my shoulder, and I focus on him again. "She loves you." His brow furrows. He must have felt me tense under his touch.

I relax and pat his shoulder gently as I walk over to Ella. She stiffens at my arrival, and I hate it.

"Alex, you must tell us a joke." Aine nods at me before returning her attention to Alex, who is basking in the attention.

I lean in and kiss Ella on the cheek. She looks up and her smile is heavy.

"Where do you find a cow with no legs?" Alex smiles, and I want to smash my fist into his mouth. What kind of stupid joke was that? I glance at Ella to find her smiling at Alex. It looks genuine.

Aine shakes her head.

Alex smiles at Ella. "Ella, you try. You're good at these."

Ella gives a short laugh. "That's such a lie." She exhales loudly as she thinks. "I don't know. In a field?"

I'm imagining if Ella wasn't with me, and I had to watch her love someone else. I think I would actually kill Alex. I couldn't accept it.

Alex laughs, and I'm looking around to see if I'm the only one who wants to strangle him. "Right where you left it," he answers and Aine laughs.

"Ella was right. They are very bad," Aine says, but her voice still sings with humor.

"Food's ready." Asher is wearing a pair of mitts on his hands and he looks happy. Are his eyes lingering on Ella and Alex?

I take her hand and her head snaps up at me in surprise.

"You hungry?" I try to drag all her attention back to me. She nods, her lashes fluttering closed. She's cutting me off, and I know whom to blame. I glance up to find Alex looking at me. I hope he sees the promise in my eyes. I will kill him if he upsets her.

His eyes fill with fear, and he scurries off to the table.

Everyone is seated, and I don't want to join them. I pause.

"You okay?" I ask Ella, tilting her face up toward me.

"I'm so tired." She sounds truthful and she looks tired.

I press my lips to hers, and some of the tension leaves my body when she kisses me back. She's mine.

We join the rest at the table. I'm very aware of how many times Alex stares over at Ella. He's testing me. I smile throughout most of the meal as I think of all the ways I can hurt him. I answer all the questions. Each time I look at Ella, I see the turmoil in her and it's killing me.

"I'm a romantic," Aine declares at the table, and she's looking at Ella. "Tell us about your first date. I love a good story."

Ella's wide green eyes stare up at me. Her cheeks burn and I wonder what she's thinking. Our first date was the picnic when I tasted her in the maze. Her face grows hotter, and I can't stop the grin.

"We had a beautiful picnic in the garden." Ella's soft voice is filled with a smile, and I want her to stay this way.

"Lucas was very charming." She glances up at me, and my grin turns into a smile.

"He gets that from me," my mother says and everyone laughs.

I don't. How would I know what parts of me are like her? I don't know her. She focuses on her dinner, when her eyes meet mine.

Ella clears her throat, and I'm aware of the change in the atmosphere around the table.

"We took a stroll in the maze." Her voice is trailing off, and it's like she regrets adding that part.

"Oh, I've never actually gone into the maze. It's caught my attention, but I would no doubt end up lost. My coordination isn't the best." Aine giggles as she sips from her glass of wine. She looks like she's been sipping from it all afternoon.

"I prefer the gardens." Ella drinks from her water, and when she looks up at me, I smile at her.

"Yes, the gardens are stunning," Alex says. "It's actually where Ella and I first met."

I grip my own glass, but I don't pick it up. I tell myself flicking it at Alex would cause too much outrage. But what's he doing? I grin at him.

"I remember that day," I say.

Ella is tense beside me.

"Oh, that's right. You arrived a while later," Alex fires back and I'm wondering if he's that fucking stupid that he thinks he can rile me up and not face the consequences.

Alex looks at Ella. "That day had started so well."

My stomach tightens when I think of what I had made Ella do that day. He was bringing it back up on purpose.

"Did it not end well?" Aine asks, her eyes dancing with alcohol.

Alex flickers a glance at me, and I hope he reads me. I'm going to hurt him if he hurts Ella.

"It did. Alex fell and tore his trousers." Ella speaks up, and I have such a proud moment that she would lie.

Alex doesn't look happy.

"It was one of your favorite suits too," Ella adds, but I can hear the quiver in her voice.

"My favorite suit was the one I wore to the ball," Alex says back, and he smiles fondly at Ella. My stomach twists.

I'm not the only one noticing Alex fawning over Ella.

"It looks like you might have some competition," Aine says with a giggle.

"I think you've had enough wine." I speak clearly and her smile slips.

"Lucas." My mother's words come out with a whoosh. Like she can't believe I just said that. She has no right to play mother now. I don't waste my breath on her.

"I think dessert would be nice." Sean speaks up, and it cracks the awkwardness.

"Excuse me." I stand after excusing myself from the table. I feel ready to explode, and I can't in front of Ella. I don't look at her as I leave the table and make my way outside.

The snow has finally stopped falling. I move to the side of the house, not wanting anyone to see me from the window. I want to kill Alex. He's pushing me too far. The back door opens, and I'm shaking my head. I don't need anyone else having a go. I'll snap.

"Lucas." Asher's voice has me remaining silent. No doubt he'll banish me from his home. I could see him rooting for Alex and Ella. *Over my dead body.*

"Lucas." He steps around the side of the house and faces me. When his eyes clash with mine, he pauses and pushes his hands into his pockets.

"Aine's scoffed two bottles of my finest wine," he says like I give a shit.

"I'm sure she can afford to replace them," I say, kicking snow, just wanting him to say what he needs to say and then leave.

"I'll have a word with Alex."

I glance at him. What's he playing at?

"About what?"

Asher takes a step closer to me, but I can see his caution. "About Ella. He's fond of her, and he knows she's with you, but him jabbing at you isn't wise. I'll have a word."

I smirk. "Ah, you don't want *me* to have a word." I see he's protecting his son, but doing it in a roundabout way.

"We got off to a bad start, but I see you will be a great leader." His words are said to the side of the house. "Don't let your temper be your downfall. I will get the same results as you, but let me talk to him."

Now Asher looks at me.

"Okay."

His smile of relief is quick. He nods while moving to the side of the house. He opens a small door and takes out two bottles of wine.

"The best type of cooler."

He holds them up with a nod. "See you inside." He leaves with his stupid notion that Alex is safe.

Not a hope.

CHAPTER TWENTY

ELLA

Since Lucas arrived back, he hasn't paid me any attention. He's watching Alex like a hawk. I want Alex to stick with the crowd, because once he leaves, I can see Lucas pouncing.

I announce I'm going to bed, and Lucas kisses me goodnight and tells me he'll be in later. This has all my alarm bells ringing. I want to ask him to leave Alex alone, but his attention is off me, and I want to use that fact.

It's wrong and selfish, but I need to get to Hannah and Jessie. My stomach twists as I climb into bed. It's going to be a long night waiting for everyone to fall asleep.

My stomach lifts as the door closes, and I can smell Lucas. The sound of material moving has me picturing him stripping. The bed dips and my heart pounds. He moves in behind me as the heat of his bare chest penetrates through my back. His large arm pulls me in closer, and I'm wrapped up in him as he kisses the crown of my head.

I can feel his erection and my body responds, but I push the need for Lucas down. I need to pretend to be asleep. I relax and I swear he's smelling me. My lips tug up.

"Ella." His voice has me going still, and I remember to breathe.

I groan and shuffle into the pillow like he disturbed me.

He kisses my head again, and his arms tighten on my waist. But he's settled more behind me.

"I love you." His words have guilt churning in my stomach at what I'm doing, but I know if I told him that I want to go get them, he wouldn't allow it. He would lock me up to stop me from getting them. So telling him isn't an option.

I lie awake in his arms as he slowly falls asleep holding me. My heart pounds each time I think of slipping out. I've stashed my clothes in the bathroom amongst the towels. I also stowed Asher's Jeep keys there. I lift Lucas's arms slowly, and he pulls me back in.

This isn't going to be easy. He pulls me even tighter as his other hand gropes my boob. Really? He's thinking about that while he sleeps? I detangle myself and slide out. I hold my breath as he moves onto his stomach. Once his breathing evens out, I tiptoe out of the room. Sweat has already gathered along my neck as I pull the door gently behind me.

The floorboard creaks under my feet, and it sounds like a gunshot went off. I close my eyes tightly and curse the noise. My heart beats too wildly in my chest, and I know I need to keep moving.

I'm picturing Lucas behind me with each step I take. I make it to the bathroom and dress quickly in all black. With my sneakers and the Jeep keys, I leave the bathroom and creep into the living room. My heart pounds. Someone is sitting at the table. They look like they're staring at me, but they don't move.

I try to calm down and focus. It's Aine. She doesn't move as I creep closer. She's asleep sitting up. My heart beats wildly as I turn and make my way to the back door. I take one final look before I push through it.

***

There are no cars on the road as I push the pedal to the floor. I have a long drive ahead of me. I will be arriving in daylight. I hate that, but I know if I'm to get out, it would have to be nighttime. The further away I get from Lucas, the sicker I feel. I'm angry that he never told me, but I'm also praying to God that he forgives me. The idea of losing him has me nearly turning back.

"Ella, who isn't Bella," I say out loud and that's what keeps me going. She would have done the same for me. To think of her and Jessie trapped in a cell under the shed has me wishing I could push the Jeep faster. I'm clocking 170, and yet I feel like I'm crawling.

Time passes funny when you're driving at night. I pass two towns before I hit the countryside again, just as the sun is rising in the distance. It feels like a timer is ringing.

Is Lucas getting up now? Does he know I was missing? My stomach twists painfully, and my chest tightens. I rub it to try to relieve some of the pain. Rolling down the window, I let the cool air keep me awake. I don't want to stop, but I also don't want to crash with tiredness. I pull in at a gas station and go to the bathroom before returning to the Jeep. It's nice to stretch my legs a little.

I root around and find some loose coins. It's enough for a coffee. I enter the self-service area and make a coffee with two sugars. I swallow the lump in my throat. *I will be back to him in a few hours*, I remind myself, as I pay for the coffee and return to the Jeep.

I sit in the car and turn the key. A ringing phone has me spilling half of the coffee across my leg. It burns.

I curse as I try to mop it up with a jacket that's in the front seat. The phone continues to ring, and I see a slick black phone beside the handbrake. *Don't answer it, Ella.*

It stops ringing and I finish cleaning myself as best I can while I drink down some of my coffee.

I nearly spill it again as the phone rings. It's like the music to my doom. Is it Lucas? Or could it be Asher? Or the cops? Would he have reported the Jeep as stolen? Oh God. I hadn't thought of that. I pick up the ringing phone and answer it.

"Ella." It's Lucas. His voice is a growl, and I can't even answer him. "Ella!"

I hang up and switch off the phone before I lose my nerve, and I start to drive again.

I pull out onto the road and continue my journey, willing myself not to feel bad.

It takes another few hours before I drive close to the house. I pull up in the gateway of a field. The phone in the middle compartment has me chewing my lip. Should I take it? In case things go wrong?

I take a deep breath and close my eyes. Nothing is going to go wrong. I'm going in there, getting Hannah and Jessie, and leaving.

It's early in the morning, so I hope that Henry sleeps in late. I close the door and lock the Jeep. Stuffing the keys into my pocket, I run across the road. I keep to the tree lines and the foliage thins out and the fencing becomes more apparent. I climb it and land on the soft grass.

My heart pounds in my ears as I run along the outskirts of the lawn. I feel like this is madness and am questioning if I'm really here. I could be back in bed, wrapped in Lucas's warmth. The thought of Lucas has my strength wavering. He's going to kill me.

The gravel under my feet has my heart racing. I'm so close to the sheds. I glance to my right and see the hot tub that sits right outside Lucas's bedroom. God, how long ago was that? It's weird being back. It gives me comfort but also strangles me with fear. The shed door creaks, but I'm elated that it isn't locked as I step into the shed.

I let my eyes adjust before I carefully move around the space. I check the shelving along the back wall, and when I spot a hammer amongst the tools, I pick it up and grip the black rubber handle. Steps are in front of me. My heart pounds loudly, and I close my eyes and try to control my body.

I need to calm myself. I rub my sweaty palms on my jeans, wiping one hand at a time before I take the first step. A noise has me growing stiff. *Thump, thump, thump.* My heart has the blood racing to my feet, and I want to curl up and make myself small. I don't know if there's more noise. The blood roars in my ears, blocking out everything else. Looking around me has me hunching my shoulders. My fear is growing, and I tell myself to move now!

The steps disappear under me as I race down them. I'm dizzy with adrenaline and start opening doors. The first is empty, the second locked, and the third door has me pausing.

A rope hangs from the ceiling, and dried red paint is splashed across the floor. I know it's not paint; I know the smell. But as I close the door, I tell myself it's paint. I swallow the bile that's rising fast up my throat and keep opening doors. Storage units, empty rooms. My heart is ready to come out of my chest. They aren't here.

I reach the last door and my stomach heaves. It's a hallway that leads off in three different directions. It's a maze. I think of Henry's maze outside. Some small voice is telling me to leave. That if I continue, there will be no way back. What horrors lie down here? I tighten my hold on the hammer as a noise behind me has me jumping. I can't look around, but I have to.

I laugh at the empty air. *It's okay. It's okay.*

Taking a deep breath, I continue down the darkened hallway. Every few feet, a light shows the way, but I can't see much behind me or ahead of me. Hope blossoms as I come across a door with bars on it. I look inside and the hope in me is crushed. It's empty.

I move past three more lights. That's seven in total. When I get Hannah and Jessie, I need to be able to find our way out of here. After three more lights—that's ten now—I notice the doors have changed. The next three are white.

My stomach squeezes painfully as I look inside the first one. I can see through a small square of glass. The space is darkened, and I swallow the saliva in my mouth. I can make out a shape. I trail my hand along the wall until I touch a switch. I press it and a scream claws its way up my throat.

CHAPTER TWENTY-ONE

ELLA

My hands collide with the piece of glass, and it rattles but doesn't shatter. I keep trying to open the door, but it won't budge.

"Jessie." Her name is strangled from me as I continue to hit the glass. She isn't moving. "Jessie."

The edge of the hammer hits the glass. I had forgotten I was holding it. I turn my head away as I shatter the glass inward.

"Jessie." I scream her name through the broken window. She doesn't move. Dropping the hammer, I pull with both hands.

"Goddamn it." It won't budge. I bring the hammer down on the door handle with all my force. The noise of steel hitting steel rings out, and I know I'm being too noisy, but the panic that's crawling along my skin has my fear reaching a level it's never reached before. It's the type of fear that makes you brave, and right now, I don't care who I attract. All I know is that I want to get Jessie to safety.

The handle hits the floor, and I slam my shoulder against the door and it gives way. Glass crunches under my feet as I run to Jessie. She's lying on the concrete floor with her back to me. She's so still. Now that I've reached her, I'm standing over her, frozen.

She's dead. She's too still. A shiver assaults my body, and I tell myself it's a bunch of clothes as I lower myself to my knees and touch her. I jump back. She's cold, so cold.

I'm scrambling backward across broken glass. Blood pools quickly, but I don't feel the pain.

"Hannah." Her name tumbles from my mouth as I rise and grab the hammer. I stumble away from Jessie.

"Hannah!" I roar the minute I leave the cell. My voice bounces off the walls and slams back into me. It's like a punch to the stomach, and I bend over, trying to control my racing heart.

A noise has me going still. It sounds further down the hall. I'm running. I hear it again. I stop at a door, and I can't believe who I'm looking at. It's Hannah and she's screaming.

"Stand back." I raise the hammer for her to see, and she quickly moves back. I don't ponder the bruises on her face or the fear in her eyes. After wiping my bloody hands on my jeans, I grip the hammer before slamming it down on the door handle. It takes two more tries before the handle hits the ground. I'm almost giddy as I slam my shoulder into the door and it bounces open.

Hannah starts crying. The hammer falls from my hand and hits the ground as she crumbles in my arms, sobbing.

"Hannah, we need to leave." My words don't penetrate her breakdown. She's fighting to breathe.

"Hannah, we need to go." I push her away and pick up the hammer. She looks at me now. "We need to leave."

She nods her head rapidly like she's coming out of a dream. I give her a smile, and she places her hand in my blood soaked one. She doesn't even notice.

"I knew you would return to me." A cold finger runs up my spine at the voice.

Hannah cries out as Henry walks into the cell. He's not wearing his glasses, and his similarities to Lucas are frightening. Raising the hammer, I tuck Hannah behind me.

"Stay away from us." Fear has me ready to do the worst. I will hit him. I know it and he knows it. He moves a bit closer, and my temperature spikes.

"I swear to God, Henry, you take one more step..." I threaten and he pauses. I move toward the door, pushing Hannah first. "Run, Hannah," I say to her, without taking my eyes off Henry.

"No, you too." She's sobbing, and I know both of us leaving isn't possible.

"I said go. I'll be right behind you." I push her, and she gives out a strangled cry before she runs.

"You really shouldn't have done that." He tilts his head while hunching.

"You killed Jessie." I tighten my hold on the hammer. Henry keeps looking behind me, and I'm tempted to look over my shoulder, but I feel like it's a trick.

I shift a bit away from the door so I can see if anyone is behind me. Nobody is there.

"I really like Hannah." He shakes his head. "She's a screamer."

I raise the hammer higher. I want to hurt him so badly. "What did you do to her?" I don't want to know. Yet, I want every detail so she doesn't have to go through it alone.

"She won't make it out of here."

A fist tightens around my heart. I start to move toward the door. Now I regret smashing the door handle. I could have locked him in here.

"Are you going to run?" His eyes shine with delight. My bones quiver.

I'm going to run. I now have my back to the open door. I'm two steps away. He moves and I don't threaten him again. I fire the hammer and run as he roars in pain. I was aiming for his face, but I think I got his arm. My legs catch and I stumble, only to push off a wall. Panic claws at me as he roars in fury. He's out of the room and moving fast. I see Hannah and I want to cry.

"Go!" I yell at her. Her eyes widen with fear as she looks over my shoulder. What is she doing? It's then I see Jessie's body propped up against the wall. She must know she's dead.

"Go, Hannah!"

I turn at the last second and swing for Henry. He's so much faster and stronger than I could have ever thought. He sidesteps me quickly and takes me to the floor. The air leaves my lungs and they won't refill. I try to turn and pull away from him. Everything in me burns. My vision grows dark, but I see Hannah's receding feet as she runs.

***

"Ella."

I try to open my eyes, but my lids are too heavy.

"Ella."

The sting across my face has my eyes snapping open. I try to move away from Henry, but he's too close. My back hits a wall.

"Wakey, wakey."

The first thing I feel is the breeze on my bare legs and arms. I look down and want to pull the white nightdress off me. He changed me.

"You were asleep a while, and I wanted you to be more comfortable."

I feel sick as I allow myself to assess other areas. I'm not sore anywhere; only my hands still burn from all the cuts. My eyes bounce back up to his.

"Where are my clothes?"

"You really hurt me." He rubs his left shoulder. The arm is hanging slightly.

"I'm glad," I say while my heart pounds.

"Your friend got away." His face twists.

I exhale a shaky breath. That's something. Hannah's safe.

"He will kill you," I say, and smile at Henry. He had to know that.

He grins back at me and it's unsettling. "He won't have a chance. The minute he comes back here, he will be locked up until he awaits his punishment. Lucas has no claim over you."

He moves closer, and I push myself deeper into the wall. "If you behave, I might ask my father if you can still be my bride."

I look away from him, my stomach twisting.

"Since I have no other options right now, I think he might agree."

A sob I'm holding in rips free from me. "I would rather face my punishment than have to be near you."

His grin dissolves, and his hands tighten around my neck. "You're a little bitch, just like the rest."

I can't breathe. I pull at his arms, but they are like a vise around me. My nails drag down his face, and he screams but doesn't release me. I beat him until I think I'm going to pass out. My hits grow weaker. His face is so red, and his eyes bulge as he squeezes the air out of my lungs.

"Oh, for goodness' sake, Henry. Can you not control yourself?"

He jumps away from me, and I gasp for air as I look up at Sandra. I choke as I stumble to her. My balance is off, and I hit the wall while gripping my throat.

"Sandra." I say her name to make sure it's really her. "You have to get me out of here," I plead as I move away from Henry, who's looking at me like I'm a wild animal. I cough, and the pain in my neck has me rubbing it.

"Why?" Sandra asks and I stop moving toward her.

"He just tried to kill me."

She doesn't flinch. "You aggravated him, when you knew you shouldn't."

"I know you're mad over Lucas…"

She raises her hand. "I'm not mad, Ella. I'm fuming. You both humiliated me."

"I'm sorry." I cough and look at Henry. He's still holding his face, and he looks at the small droplets of blood on his fingers.

"When I was informed that you arrived back, I wanted to personally tell you myself that your punishment will be severe and that I will have Lucas. His banishment can be lifted with a click of my fingers." She clicks her fingers together for emphasis.

"He killed Jessie." I point at Henry. She has to understand that this isn't just a punishment; he's a murderer. For the first time, I see some humanity in her eyes.

She looks at him and he shrugs. "Did you have to do that?" She speaks to him like she's talking to a child, and I'm wondering if she knows how dangerous he is.

"I want you to go. I need to talk to Ella alone." Henry whines like he didn't just try to kill me.

I'm shaking my head, and I'm ready to cling to Sandra.

"Please, please, don't leave me."

She moves quickly and pulls the cell door closed behind me. Horror roars through me, and I race to the bars.

"What are you doing?" A key turns and Henry stands up. I'm shaking my head.

"Sandra, nonononono! Don't leave me."

She's looking me dead in the eye.

"Open the door," Henry barks behind me, and the horror of what she's doing has a grin growing on her face.

"Enjoy your time together."

I throw myself at the door, and Sandra jumps back at the impact.

"Let me out!"

Sandra's eyes grow wide, and she turns on her heel and runs. I'm screaming and slamming my fists against the door until there's nothing left in me.

"This is your fault." My sobs cut off as I slowly turn around to Henry. He's right behind me, and bile crawls up my throat.

"Henry," I plead.

He grins.

I'm staring into the face of doom.

CHAPTER TWENTY-TWO

LUCAS (BEFORE)

I wake up with a raging hard-on and feel around for Ella. Her side of the bed is empty. Raising my head from the pillow, I start to wake up slowly. She isn't here. My body aches with tiredness.

I never got Alex on his own last night. Each time I tried, George or his father were there hovering around him like guardian angels. He soaked up all the attention. If Alex had power, he would be ruthless. It would go straight to his head, and he wouldn't know when to stop taking. That's all I see each time I look at him.

I roll out of bed, and I'm tempted to relieve myself. Where was Ella? My shaft grows harder as I think of her under me. I wake up a little more and try to move my bulge before pulling on a pair of jeans. I take out a fresh red T-shirt and sling it over my shoulder while reaching down and grabbing my boots and socks.

The bathroom is empty as I finish washing and pulling on my T-shirt. I carry my boots out into the living room. The coffee smell is nice to wake up to.

"Morning," my mother sings while holding up a red cup. "Can I make you one?" she asks.

I grumble a no as I look around for Ella, but I don't see her. After sitting down, I pull on my socks.

Asher is in the kitchen. Sean and George are seated at the table. My eyes land on Aine. She looks like she's nursing the mother of all hangovers.

"Sunglasses inside?" I fire at her and grin.

She waves me off, mumbling something incoherent.

It's then I notice Alex isn't here either. I'll kill him. The minute my back is turned, he's chasing after Ella.

"Has anyone seen Ella and Alex?" I ask as I tie my laces. When I look up, I don't like the troubled look I see on Asher's face.

"I thought they were still sleeping."

I stand and Asher turns away from me. I'm moving down the hall, rechecking the bathroom that I just used. The bathroom is empty. When I return to the room, I see her sneakers are gone. She must be outside. I grab a jumper before heading out back.

The snow is almost gone, and green grass sprouts up through the melting patches. I do a full three-sixty and I can't see her.

"Ella!" I call as I walk to the tree line. I don't walk deep into the forest as I call her name, and when she doesn't respond, I tell myself to relax. It's cold as I walk back to the house, stuffing my hands into my pockets to warm my fingers. I race back up the steps and enter the house. There's a commotion in the kitchen that ceases the moment I enter.

Alex looks like he just woke up. His eyes are wide, as he stares at me. No one speaks.

"Asher's Jeep is missing. He thought Alex was up earlier and that he had gone to the shop."

My stomach wrings painfully as my mother speaks to me.

"Right?" I ask slowly, but deep in the back of my mind, I'm adding it up.

"Someone took it, Lucas." My mother's words aren't measured.

She wouldn't, I keep telling myself. Why would she take the Jeep? I knew something was wrong yesterday.

"Alex has something to say." Asher speaks up while stepping closer to his son.

"What did you do?" I'm clearing a path to him. All I see is him leaning into Ella yesterday as he whispered in her ear while the snow fell around them.

"He did nothing wrong." Asher jumps to his son's defense, but I don't see him. I see Alex.

I push him aside and grip Alex by the throat. I'm moving until he's up against the kitchen cabinet. "What did you do?" I shake him and all the color leaves his face.

His father grabs my arm. "Let my son go." His hands dig into my arm, trying to pull my hands from his son's throat.

"Lucas." My mother's pleas bounce off me as I shake Alex again, my thumb pushing into his windpipe.

"What did you do?"

His mouth opens and closes. Asher pushes against my arm with all his strength, and I loosen my hold.

"She was asking about Hannah and Jessie," Alex says.

My hand slips from Alex's throat, and his father grabs him as he slumps while coughing and sputtering for air.

I turn to the others, each face filled with horror.

"I couldn't lie to her." Alex speaks through deep breaths.

She asked me if I had anything else to tell her. I lied to her.

I turn back to Alex, and his father and Sean block me.

"You knew she was leaving?"

Asher's shoulders hunch like he's waiting on a blow. Guilt fills Alex's eyes.

"If anything happens to her, I'm going to kill you." My words are calm. A calm starts to settle on me. I nod. "I will kill you with my bare hands."

"There's a phone in the Jeep."

Asher's words have my heart pounding. "Ring it." What is he still standing there for?

"Ring it," I repeat and clench my fists, stopping myself before I drag him to a phone. He moves and I'm on his heels.

He picks up a phone and jabs in a number. He needs to move faster. He looks up at me. "I can't breathe with you on top of me."

I take a step back as the phone rings. It rings and rings, and I glare at Alex, who's being nursed by my mother.

I sneer at her. "Some mother you are," I bite at her, and she recoils away from me like she can outrun my words.

"Maybe everyone needs to calm down." Aine pulls off her sunglasses, and her bloodshot eyes meet mine.

I glare at Asher, and he swallows as he puts the phone down. "No answer."

I move back into his space. "Try again." He dials the number, and I rip the phone from his hand.

"She could have gone to the shop," Aine rambles behind me.

I clutch the phone tighter in my hand. It's ringing, and my heart is ready to come out of my chest when someone answers.

"Ella." Silence on the other end. It's like the room is holding its breath.

"Ella," I shout and the phone goes dead. I'm staring at the receiver before I slam it back down.

"Ring again," I command and Asher does quickly.

His eyes waver as he replaces the receiver. "It's off." I have to walk away before I attack him. I can't think straight.

"Let's go." George jingles keys at me, and I'm on his heels.

"I want to come." Alex has me making a detour from the door and toward him. He backs up into the wall. Everyone is moving at once.

"You will never be in the same space as her again." I'm breathing heavily as I look down at him.

I'm walking away because I don't have time to waste.

"I'll drive," I say to George as he climbs into the driver seat.

"No." He closes the door and glances at me through the window. There's apprehension in his eyes. I get into the passenger seat and close the door before buckling my belt just as the back door opens. I spin, ready to pull Alex out of the car.

My mother looks at me before buckling herself in.

"Get out," I bark. I don't want to be trapped in a car with her.

"Drive, George." Her commanding voice has me unbuckling my belt.

"Lucas." It's George's voice of reason that has me facing forward. He drives away immediately, as if he fears I'll change my mind. Being stuck in a car with my mother for this journey may be a torture I deserve.

I roll down the window, and all I want right now is for someone to anesthetize me so I don't have to feel. I close my eyes and think back to my lesson with my father. I need to numb myself or I won't last this journey.

"She's a clever girl. I'm sure she's fine." My eyes snap open at my mother's words. I don't dare look back at her. I grip the handle above my head to give my hands something to strangle.

"I must admit, I'm a bit surprised with how easily she manipulated you and Alex."

I release the handle, and it flips up with a bang as I turn to her. "That's great, Elizabeth. Fantastic way to rebuild bridges with your son. Insult the woman I'm going to marry."

"It's not an insult, Lucas. It's a compliment. She uses her beauty to get what she wants. That's not a bad thing."

I sneer at her. "She has no idea of her beauty. That's what makes her beautiful. So you have it all wrong." I face forward in my seat, already regretting engaging in conversation with her. "This isn't a therapy session or an analysis. So I'd appreciate"—I'm aware of George tensing, his fingers tightening around the steering wheel, so I keep the you shut the fuck up to myself—"if you stay quiet."

Silence falls around the car, and I bathe in it and the numbness for the next two hours. Every few minutes, my stomach tightens, and I shift in my seat to settle it.

"These girls are her friends?" My mother starts talking again, and I close my eyes. Two hours of peace may have been two seconds. Her voice grates through me.

"No. She hates them. That's why she ran off to save them." I knew this is exactly what would happen if she found out about Hannah and Jessie. I just thought she would never find out about them.

"Sarcasm is another form of anger, Lucas. I'm not the enemy."

I'd heard Asher say that before about Alex, and he was wrong.

"I'm just trying to understand. She will be my daughter-in-law."

I'm facing my mother again. "Is this why you came? To torture me?"

Her lips draw a straight line, and it's the first time I've seen her pissed. "I came because this is the only opportunity I have to spend time with my son."

Guilt twists my stomach. "You picked a really bad time, Elizabeth." I sit forward.

"I'm your mother, not Elizabeth." Her angry words have me scrubbing a hand across my face.

"We need to talk about our plan for getting Ella out." George pulls me out of the padded cell I felt my mother pushing me into. I roll down the window and unbuckle my belt. It's starting to feel constricting.

"Could you roll up the window? It's very cold back here."

I press the button, and the window closes.

"Thank you."

"Both of you wait in the car. I'll go get her," I say. That's the plan. I don't need to be worrying about more people.

"Lucas, the moment you step onto that property, he will know, and he won't let you go a second time."

I run my hands through my hair. George is right. Walking in there isn't going to be easy.

Maybe she got Hannah and Jessie out. I know it's a lie. They're in Henry's hands, and that reduces the odds of them getting out safely to nearly nonexistent.

A ripple races under the surface of my skin. *Fear.* What if I lose her? I allow myself to open my mind to that possibility before I turn it off as quickly as I turned it on.

"What do you suggest?" I glance at George.

"Let me go in. They won't suspect me. I told Mark I was sick with the flu. They have no idea where I went."

I don't want to see anything bad happen to George. Henry already doesn't like him. "I don't think I can risk you, George," I answer honestly.

"Let me," my mother chimes in from the back.

I want to say, *Go ahead. I can risk you*, but the reality is, I don't want to lose her again.

"No," I say and she doesn't fight me on it.

We still have a long way to go before I get to Ella.

Hold on. I'm coming.

CHAPTER TWENTY-THREE

ELLA

Henry moves to the other side of the cell and slowly sits on the ground. The violence that shone in his eyes only moments ago is gone. I'm still banging on the door, screaming for Sandra to come back.

"Stop."

I don't know how many times Henry has asked me to stop, but my hands fall to my sides as I glance at him. My throat aches and burns from screaming.

"Stop." He says it gently as he takes his glasses from his pocket and slides them on. He smiles up at me. "That's better. A vision in white."

I swallow bile and keep my back to the wall. My mind can't fully accept that I'm locked in a cell with Henry.

"I knew you would come back." He looks at the door before he glances at me. "They all come back." He exhales loudly. "I think when you spend time with me, you will really like me, Ella."

He's out of his mind. I keep listening, praying that Sandra doesn't really leave me here. She can't. She won't.

The hallway is different. It's nicer and I don't get the smell of earth, like in the cell I was in before. I was in a different part of the house. I inch closer to the door. My hands ache and I loosen my fists. I glance at Henry.

"Where am I?" He must have moved me when I was knocked out. He must have changed me too. I shiver and wrap my arms around my waist.

Henry hasn't taken his eyes off me, and knowing he is gay is the only thing that's keeping some of my fear at bay. If I didn't know that, I don't think I would be able to function with how he's looking at me right now.

"In the most important part of the house." He rises and so does my heart rate. I loosen my hands and let them fall to my side before I feel the wall behind me.

My palms grow slick with sweat, but he doesn't come closer to me. "This is my father's playground. It's also where meetings are held and punishments performed. In the 'box.'" He does air quotes around the word box.

If Andrew found us, what would he do? He locked his own wife up. What would he do to someone like me?

"Sandra has surprised me." He steps away from the wall, and I push my back as deep as the concrete wall will allow, which isn't far at all.

"She has also disappointed me." He wags his fingers while he hunches.

He smiles and pushes his glasses up on his nose. "I always take the positive in every situation." He takes a step toward me.

I shake my head. I could never fight him. I'm not strong enough. "Please, Henry," I whimper.

"Me and you have time to bond." He reaches me, and as his finger prods my cheek, I whimper more. He keeps prodding my cheek. Each prod has my skull connecting with the wall. It's not hard enough to hurt me, but it's sending waves of fear shooting down my body.

"I like you, Ella. There's something so enticing about breaking you."

My heart stalls before it gallops.

He laughs and steps away from me. "You should see your face." He makes a monstrous face with wide eyes and a gaping mouth. He laughs at himself and shakes his head.

"I don't mean breaking your bones. I do that all the time, and honestly"—he looks at me—"it gets boring." He laughs as he walks around the small cell. "That's a lie. It never bores me."

I'm straining to see out of the bars in the door. Someone has to come. My lungs contract painfully. Maybe having Andrew find us would be easier than this.

"Do you know what I really like about you?" He's back in front of me. He's so much taller, and it reminds me how weak I am right now. How vulnerable I am.

"You're a listener." He sounds sincere. He pokes my cheek again, only this time he digs his finger into my cheek until the pain brings tears to my eyes. He stops poking me.

"Why do you prefer Lucas over me?"

The question is like a punch in the gut. There's no answer to that. If I lie, he'll see it. I shrug. "I don't know."

He pokes my chest. "Don't tell me lies."

My throat tightens and I close my eyes to keep down the fear that's cutting off all rational thought from my brain.

"He's kind," I whisper and open my eyes.

Henry nods. "I don't see that," he says honestly. "What else?"

I want to beg him to stop. I don't want to do this with him. It's like running across a field filled with grenades. One wrong step, and I'm dead.

"Don't lie." He pokes my chest harder this time. My back collides with the wall. Pain from when he tackled me to the ground erupts. I think of Hannah. She's free.

"He's protective," I say and my chest aches with a longing like I've been apart from Lucas for years. I have no idea how much time has passed. My mouth is dry, and I swear I've been drugged. I could have been here for hours or days. I have no idea.

Henry bobs his head from left to right. "What do you like about me?"

My lips tremble, and I chew on my jaw until blood fills my mouth. What quality can I find in Henry? None.

"What do you dislike about me?" He quickly throws in the question.

Everything.

"I don't know." I shake my head, and his palm presses against my chest. I'm picturing my chest caving in around his hand. "Henry, please," I whimper again.

He smiles. His eyes move to my lips, and I can't stop the horror that enters me. "I've never kissed a girl," he admits.

I'm shaking my head. Everything inside turns to jelly, and I have nothing left in me.

"Please," I plead one final time.

He smiles. "You sound just like your mother."

"What?" My nerves all spark to life at once.

He grins. "Because I like you so much, I'll tell you. Right now, she's being tortured in her home."

Everything in me roars to get out. He's lying. He has to be. I'm shaking my head like I can banish his words.

Henry lets me go easily, and I grip the bars and scream at the top of my lungs for help. He isn't expecting it, and I get three roars in before he grabs me around the waist with one arm and covers my mouth with the other hand, cutting off my screams. I kick out and make contact, but my bare feet don't do any damage. I sink my teeth into his hand,

and he lets my mouth go. I can't stop the frenzy of panic as I claw and kick at Henry.

My back painfully hits the floor, the air torn from me, and he's on top of me. I'm waiting for him to kill me. The savagery in his eyes has me fighting. I scream as he slams my arms down and holds them.

"Shut up!" Spit flicks across my face as he roars. A piece of me shrivels and I sob. He's breathing heavy into my neck, and I picture myself somewhere far away. My mother. I sob again. What's happening to her?

"Everyone is dying..." He's breathing heavier along my neck, and I want him off me, but I don't dare move a muscle.

"It's because of you that everyone is being hurt. Because you won't submit."

Henry leaves my neck, and his face moves too close to mine. "I know what it feels like to fight against what makes you up. The part of you that is so drawn to someone. It's like someone trying to make you walk on your hands. If I ask you to forget Lucas, it will be hard, but together, we can do it."

He exhales loudly. "It's the same for me, Ella." He looks down at me again. "I like men."

My stomach tightens. Why is he telling me this?

"But I'm willing to submit to walking on my hands for now."

Everything turns sour and I feel so heavy all of a sudden. His eyes flicker to my lips. I don't see lust. I see a test. I see curiosity.

"You understand?"

I'm going to get sick. "No," I whisper.

He nods like that's a reasonable answer. "You need to submit to me and let Lucas go. That way no one else gets harmed. I will submit to you and let my want for a man go." He speaks it really slowly.

"Submit to me, Ella."

If I say yes, will all this end? He'll know if I lie. Can I really say yes? Everyone would be safe. I close my eyes.

"Yes," I whisper.

"Look at me and say it."

I open my eyes and think of Hannah, smiling on that first day as we both stared up at the painting of Lucas. I think of Lucas's touch, love, and grin. My mother's warmth, hugs, and love fill me up. I picture Jessie lying on my bedroom floor reading a book. I think of all the perfect moments with them.

"Yes." A tear leaks from the corner of my eye and he smiles.

The press of his lips against mine stops the air in my lungs. I don't react either way, and he leans out and nods with a smile, like it wasn't so bad. Everything in me is crawling.

He's off me in a second. "That changes everything." He reaches out a hand to help me up. My hand shakes as I place it in his. He pulls me quickly and lets me go. I move back to the wall as he digs his hand into his pocket. My hands are bleeding again, and I wipe the blood on my nightdress.

"Ella, Ella." My eyes snap to Henry's. He's looking at the blood on my nightdress.

"Why did you do that? You looked so pretty." He's taking a few steps toward me. I want him to stop. I don't want him near me.

"I'll need new clothes. I want to wash." I keep my chin high and pray to God that my instincts are telling me I'm right. I need to act like I've submitted to him, like I'm not afraid even when I'm weak with fear. I have the oddest desire to curl up in a ball and let my body sleep.

He pauses and hunches his shoulder. I can tell I made the right call when he nods and takes something from his pocket.

It's a key.

My mind can't make sense of this. "You have a key?" The words dribble from my numb lips.

He smiles. "Of course. It's my just-in-case key." He grins. You never know when someone will push you into the cell, so I had a key made that opens all the doors." He taps the side of his head. "Clever, I know." His face is stretched into a crazy, huge smile.

I swallow the saliva in my mouth.

Movement outside has Henry sliding the key back into his pocket. He smiles at me as he places a finger over his lips for me to remain quiet.

"Did you get your pound of flesh?" Sandra asks. "I gave you enough time." She smiles at Henry, and he makes me jump as he walks to the door and bangs it. Sandra flinches, but the door gives her a false sense of strength.

"I will let you out, but I'm taking Ella with me. I want her punished for sleeping with my husband. So I've been studying the rules, and I discovered something very interesting. I can remove her finger. So that's what I will be doing. I will be removing your finger." She sings the last part for me.

I hear her words, but I can't understand that level of hate. He isn't her husband. Why are all these people so crazy?

Henry smiles over at me, and I can't respond. "Ella is now going to be my wife."

Sandra's laughter is loud. Her red lips tug up as she stares at Henry through the bars.

"Ella will never be yours, Henry. You aren't stupid. You have to know she will run back to Lucas."

Henry swings around to me, and I'm shaking my head as he pushes his glasses up on his face.

"She doesn't understand that we both struggle," I say and he looks back to Sandra. I'm pleading with her, pleading with my eyes not to do this. Just let us out. He's beyond volatile, and if he senses my lie, he'll kill me in a second.

"Yeah, you don't understand me and Ella."

Henry removes the key from his pocket slowly. Sandra doesn't notice as she laughs. He slides it into the door.

"I can't let you out, Henry, until you promise me that you'll drop this notion of Ella and hand her over. I gave you time with her." She blinks at me, and I wonder if she knows he's gay and that her beauty won't help her out in this situation.

Henry exhales loudly. "I've come to a very important decision." He turns the key and I look up at Sandra. She's grinning at him.

"Sandra," I warn as he pulls the door open and grabs her. Her smile vanishes as he rams his fist into her stomach. I force myself back to the wall as blood starts to pour from her, and I don't understand until I see the glint of a knife that he holds in his hands.

"You don't understand," he tells her as he plunges the knife in again, and she falls to the ground. Blood pools fast around her, and a blonde curl soaks up the blood like a sponge. I can't move. I can't breathe. Henry kneels down over her.

Move, Ella.

I'm backing slowly out the door as Henry continues to stab her still frame. He's talking to her, and he's so wrapped up in what he's doing that he doesn't notice me leaving. I'm running blindly. Tears blur my vision as I stumble into a room that holds a huge glass box with a chair in the center. I'm spinning, looking for a door

"Ella."

My name being called has me racing to a darkened corner with steps. My chest aches for air. It aches for freedom.

"Ella."

I scramble into the corner and hold as still as I can as Henry steps into the space. I want to cover my mouth. He's soaked in Sandra's blood. Tears stream down my face.

"Ella!"

I tighten my eyes as he roars my name. My body is telling me to run, but I know if I move a muscle, I'll never see the light of day again.

"Ella!" His rage has me clamping down on the inside of my mouth. He turns and races back the way he came, and I know this is the only chance I will ever get. I don't think as I race up the steps.

CHAPTER TWENTY-FOUR

ELLA

The cold concrete under my hands penetrates my skin and worms its way into my veins. Small pebbles feel harsh against the sensitive area of my hands as I scramble up the steps. All I can focus on is two black wooden doors ahead of me.

Freedom, they scream.

My bare foot slips on the edge of a step in my haste to get away from the madness behind me. My chin takes the impact of my fall as it hits the concrete slab. I don't stop as a metallic taste fills my mouth. I need to reach those doors before he reaches me.

My palms cry out as I slam them repeatedly against the black doors, but they don't budge. My frantic heart spikes my temperature, sending the cold that I briefly felt racing away. A sob I can't keep down trembles on my lips before it forms fully. I blink, allowing the tears to fall as I push with my shoulder.

Something shifts under me, and the smallest breeze that escapes the crack of the door has me pushing harder. With every ounce of strength I have, I manage to get the doors open and spring from the basement.

Grass still covered in dew blankets my feet as I race across the front lawn. I don't dare look back. I don't dare let that final image flood my mind. I want to scream for help. I want to beg someone to help me. But no one is around. Holding up my bloodied white nightgown, I continue my race for freedom across the lawn that feels more like an endless meadow. The wind whips hair across my face. The feel of it is frozen and harsh against my skin.

My fingers dig into the wooden fence as I pull myself over it. The shouts from the house, along with lights being turned on along the porch, have my heart fluttering, and my vision tinges with black along the edges. Dread pools in my stomach as I fear I might pass out. The shouts mingle with the blood that pounds in my ears as I fall across the fence and onto a hard surface. My fingers race across the tarmac.

A road.

I'm on a road. Standing, I wobble as I spin around. More tarmac, more trees. My tongue feels heavy in my mouth, and I wonder when it was that I last had something to drink. I can't remember. My feet start to move again.

I freeze. The noise of someone coming has the blood running cold in my veins. My chin scrapes against the tarmac as I throw myself down on the ground. Fear is consuming me, something I can't control, and my vision blurs and wavers. Feet appear out onto the road. A whimper pulls at me, and I close my eyes tightly. Warm liquid rushes down my face.

He can't see me. He can't see me.

My skin crawls, and I'm too afraid to open my eyes. Another part of me wants to scream so this will end. I open my eyes slowly and the feet race past me. My heart hammers in my chest as I wait for them to stop and come back, but they don't. The whimper leaves my chattering lips.

Get up, Ella.

Pushing myself up on shaky arms, I spring from the ditch and start to run in the opposite direction than the other person went. My eyes shoot around the landscape as my mind tries to push the images back in front of me. Like a detective sliding a gruesome image in front of the murderer to make him crack.

He wants me to break.

He wants to break me.

My lungs burn as I race around a bend in the road. I don't know how long I've been running for, but I haven't seen a car. My mind won't decide if that's a good thing or a bad thing.

Thin red lips. I cover my mouth to keep the scream in, the scream that's building inside me and wants out.

The noise of a vehicle cracks through my thoughts, and without slowing down, I throw my body to the left of the road, where most of the undergrowth is. My skin burns from the sharp thorns that pierce my skin and drink my blood.

As I lie still once again, the cold ground becomes comforting. It reminds me that I'm out here and not in there with that monster.

The one blonde curl wrapped in red, stained in blood. I tighten my eyes as my mind tries to conjure the rest of the image.

Move, Ella.

I leave the road completely and start to run across an open field.

Help me.

My frantic mind won't slow as my feet dig deep into the grass. I don't remember how I got here, but when I stop and look up, I'm standing outside my house.

"Mam." My lip trembles as I cry out for my mother. My body shakes and dips like it's giving up. I'm a yard from my own front door. A yard from my home.

"Mam." I shout louder as I find the use of my legs and start to run.

"Mam." My roar is said with a pounding heart. How long has it been—weeks, months, a year?

"MAM!" My fists hit the door. The overhead porch light burns my eyes from the darkness of the night.

"Mam." My cries grow, and when the door opens, I collapse on my knees at my mother's feet.

"Larry!" she shouts before she joins me on the floor. "Ella, look at me."

I do and I push her away.

"Did he hurt you?" I'm shaking, reaching for her. She doesn't look hurt. "Are you alone?"

"Larry." My mother's worried voice wavers, and she moves around me and closes the front door.

"Is someone here?" I shout at her. She needs to answer me.

My mother blinks. "Just Larry. Ella, you have to calm down." Her eyes roam across me. "Where are you hurt?" She's fighting for control, and I try to think.

"I don't know." A sob rips from me, and reality sinks in. I'm racing back to the door and locking it.

"Check all the windows," I shout at my mother. Larry enters the room. "Larry, check the back door."

He's staring at me, along with my mother.

"He's going to come here!" I roar at them. They have no idea.

The kitchen is exactly as I remember. I pull out the knife drawer and grab three large knives.

"We need to be ready." I blink the tears out of my eyes.

"Ella, what happened?" My mother's eyes waver with fear. "You're safe now." She takes an unsure step toward me.

"We aren't." I need Lucas. The Jeep has that phone in it. I can ring back the number that rang me. I leave my mother and Larry and run up to my room holding all the knives.

"Ella, tell me what's happening. Where have you been? Everyone has been looking for you. Where did all the blood come from?" My mother races behind me, and I enter my room. Leaving the knives on my bed, I pull off my nightdress.

Her inhale is sharp, and I glance in the mirror at my back. It's already bruising. I see the bruises along my arms and stomach. It must have been from when Henry slammed me down on the ground. Fresh blood keeps welling up from my hands.

I curse them.

"Ella." My mother touches my arm gently. "Please tell me what happened."

I take a deep breath. Larry enters my room, and I don't care that I'm standing in my underwear.

"Henry." I sob on his name. "He's going to kill me, and you, and everyone I love."

"Master Andrew's son?" Larry asks.

I don't have time to explain this to them.

"Larry, ring Master Andrew," my mother says.

I nearly tackle Larry to the ground to stop him from leaving the room. My mother drags me off Larry, and the sting across my face has everything in me growing silent. She just hit me.

"Calm down." She's breathing heavily, and she holds my face as I sit on the ground. "I need you to calm down," she repeats. "We won't ring anyone, I promise. Just tell me what happened."

I blink up at her. I have no idea on where to start.

"Lucas." I say his name on a wobbly smile. "I found Lucas," I tell her. She will be so happy.

My mother takes my hands in hers. Her eyes fill, but tears don't spill. Larry gets up slowly, but I keep a track on him so he doesn't leave the room.

"He's lovely," I say.

She nods. "Did he hurt you?"

Her words are like a bucket of cold water. "No. Henry hurt me. Andrew hurt me," I admit and she nods like she understands but she doesn't. I need to stay calm. I need to get to Lucas. I can see it in my mother's eyes; she thinks I lost my mind.

"Larry, why don't you ring the doctor." She ushers him with her hand while looking at me.

"I don't need a doctor." I rise and I don't want Larry to leave the room.

"Henry tried to kill me. If they figure out where I am…" I trail off. "He said he was torturing you." I sob again as I close my eyes.

My mother's warmth surrounds me, and I lean on her as she speaks. "I'm fine. No one hurt me. I think you need to rest, Ella."

I swallow and push away. "I have to find Lucas." My mind won't settle.

"Lucas?" My mother repeats. "Lucas is away with his soon-to-be-bride, Sandra." My mother's eyes grow sadder and I laugh.

"That's what they're telling people."

Her mouth twists. "Ella O'Leary. Now you stop this right now. Master Andrew explained you have been unwell." She points at me now. "You aren't well."

I laugh again, because why not? "Sandra is dead." Tears spill. "Henry killed her."

I have to turn away from my mother and calm myself. "Okay. Okay. I'm sorry." I don't know how else to deal with this situation. "I'm tired," I say, and she comes to me like it's the first time I've made sense.

"Let me help you." She smiles at me, and for a moment, I allow myself to believe it will be okay.

"What happened to your hands?" She holds them.

I hate how weak I feel. "Jessie." I swallow around the lump.

My mother nods encouragingly for me to continue.

"Jessie is dead."

My mother drops my hands. "He was telling the truth. You're unwell." The devastation on my mother's face cuts deep.

"Did you know about what goes on in that house? How they punish people?" I'm wondering what my mother sent me into.

She shakes her head. "I was hoping he was lying." She's still stuck on Master Andrew's lies.

"Why did my dad take his life?"

She flinches, and I don't want to hurt her; I want someone to tell me the truth. I'm surrounded by lies and more lies.

"Why would you ask me that?"

My heart palpitates, and it does that funny thing where it skips a beat. "Are we in financial debt?" My mother's paling face is all I need to know.

"You shouldn't have lied to me."

"I didn't. I was protecting you. I wanted you to have your fairy tale."

"Do I look like I've had a fairy tale?" I can feel the anger and panic rising in me.

Movement on the stairs has my eyes widening as I look to my mother. "Who did you call?"

Fear clutches my throat, and I have nowhere to go as Larry appears in the doorway and nods at my mother. My vision darkens.

"Hello, Ella. Everyone has been looking for you." Lucas's father smiles as he steps into my bedroom.

CHAPTER TWENTY-FIVE

ELLA

"Hello, Ella. Everyone has been looking for you." His smile shines out of all the faces he wears.

"Thank you for coming, Master Andrew." My mother bobs her head.

Red-hot rage courses through me; the betrayal burns my heart.

"You have made quite the mess." He dances closer to me. The knives on the bed are near, but I don't move.

"How did she get out? My daughter needs better care." My mother clutches her neck, and for the first time, I see the pure fear in her. She believes I'm ill. He's doing the same thing to me that he did to his wife. Did she fight and scream, plead her innocence?

"I do apologize. She attacked a staff member and got out."

My mother inhales sharply. "I hope the person is alright."

Lucas's father's eyes land on me, and it's like he sheds all his skin. "Ella." My name is said with a fondness, and my hands shake.

"I know this is all confusing to you, but you had a breakdown."

I want to spit on him, but I don't move as my heart hammers away.

"Why did she have a breakdown? I don't understand." My mother is shaking her head. I peek at Larry, who blocks the door. His eyes won't hold mine. He thinks I'm mad too.

"Ella, don't you remember?" He sounds so sincere. Why does he sound sincere? Tears burn my eyes and dry up. I remember.

"You killed Declan and Sorcha. You hit me." I touch my face. "Jessie's dead and so is Sandra." I swallow the bile as I think of Henry butchering her.

"Ella!" my mother sounds horror filled.

Andrew shakes his head. "She's confused. Don't be angry. Her mind is fractured."

He turns to me, and I don't understand how he seems so normal. "Ella, sweetheart. You had a breakdown and have been in the hospital for the last two weeks."

I'm shaking my head, but already, doubt is working its way into my mind. What he's saying sounds like a perfect solution to the madness I witnessed.

"Hannah and Jessie…"

He exhales. "Are at home and safe. Hannah has applied to colleges to be a doctor."

My legs shake. She told me that. I become aware of my nakedness. I can't look at my mother. I feel the humiliation burning my cheeks.

"Henry hurt me." Why does my body feel so raw?

Once again, Andrew takes a step toward me. "You and Henry." He turns to my mother. "I kept a certain amount of information from you."

I can see the sharp rise and fall of my mother's chest. I want to grab Andrew. I want to know. I want to know what he isn't saying. I want this to make sense.

"Ella slept with my son."

Horror fills my mother's eyes and I nod, confirming what Andrew said. It's true and I don't regret it.

"Oh, Ella." She's shaking her head in disapproval. I want to say it's okay. I'll marry Lucas.

"Henry should have known better."

"Henry? I slept with Lucas." I glance at the knives. He's lying about everything.

"Lucas is with Sandra." It's my mother's shout that fractures my heart.

"I'm not crazy," I shout back, but I feel crazy. I'm down the rabbit hole, and they're filling it in with clay.

"Sandra is dead. Henry butchered her." I cover my mouth. "All the blood." Bile crawls back up my throat.

He shakes his head, wearing that same soft expression. "I'm so sorry, Ella, but Lucas is with Sandra right now."

Not my Lucas. I'm back in the forest when he places the stone in my hand. *"Remember this place," he told me.* Tears fall down my face.

"But the cabin with the snow."

"I can't..." My mother's sobs snap me out of my memory. I want to go to her, hold her.

"Please, Master Andrew, help her."

He holds up his hand. "The cabin was a dream, Ella. Who else was there?"

"Alex, Elizabeth, Aine, Sean, George, and Asher."

He flinches at Asher's name and then smiles. "Oh, Ella. Was your mother there too?"

"What?" I swallow. "No. She's right here." I point at her and he nods.

"Sean and Aine are in the house right now at a meeting." He looks over at my mother. "I'm sure George is pouring some tea." He looks at me. "No one is trying to hurt you. You must see this isn't real."

My body starts to tremble, and all I see is Jessie's dead body and Sandra's blood. Hannah got away. Henry's lips pressed against mine. Lucas had a coffee with me on the porch. The motel was real.

"We stayed in a motel." I swallow, grappling for some sort of sense in all this.

"This ends now, Master Andrew." My mother's anger overtakes her upset.

"This isn't real," Master Andrew says. "I'm so sorry. Let me help you."

I close my eyes as I dance in the snow with Lucas. He hums off-key, and I smile as my eyes burn. ,"We danced in the snow."

So much pity leaks from my mother's eyes. I feel so broken. Is he even real? Did I create a fairy tale? He's perfect and magical.

My prince.

"I could never forget you, Lucas." I told him that in the forest. I hiccup and my legs feel weak. He was too perfect, and the rest was too devastating to be real. I'm nodding. The pain is resting on my neck and bowing my head.

The snow was heavy on the limbs of the trees as I spoke to Alex.

"None of it was real." Andrew speaks again.

I frown. "It felt so real. He felt so real."

My mother is beside me now, and I let her dress me as some part of me shuts down and goes to that place with Lucas. Each touch felt seared into my skin. The red blood on his lips.

"I tasted his blood," I tell my mother and her face is overcome with sadness.

She takes my face in her hands, and my lips tremble. "Please stop, Ella." She kisses my forehead, and she feels so real.

"Is this real?" I ask.

My mother won't look at me as she sits me on the bed. Larry immediately removes the knives like I might hurt my mother.

Lucas drinks me in as I stand in the motel room.

"You really like black," I said.

"It's my new favorite color." He took a step toward me.

"I thought it was already your favorite color."

He reached me and exhaled loudly. "It's my new favorite color on you."

I think I don't mind going there to him. Anything is more bearable than what's happening right now.

My mother places shoes on my feet. "Master Andrew, I'm coming. I want to help take care of my daughter."

"That's not necessary. The best of care will be given to her."

"With all due respect, Master Andrew, I don't have much faith in the care she was given. My daughter is bruised and terrified. Her hands are all cut. Who is going to explain all that to me?"

I keep my eyes closed as each shove and push from Henry hits my body again. I'm remembering Jessie's still frame on the ground as I smash in the glass. None of it was real, but my body begs to differ.

"She hurt herself escaping. She was hysterical. It won't happen again." Andrew's tone sounds firmer, and I open my eyes.

"Ella, I'm going to give you something to relax." He smiles at me and I nod. That sounds nice. He approaches me, and I close my eyes.

"You made him read the Bible." I speak up to Andrew as warmth enters my veins. I'm thinking of the day in the motel room. "You said he should know his enemies."

There's a pause in Andrew's stature, and he looks at me like he's seeing me for the first time.

"He was looking for a loophole." I laugh, but it sounds kind of garbled.

I'm standing with the aid of Andrew, and everything feels warm. "Henry killed his dog," I tell Andrew, and he nods at me before turning to my mother.

"This won't happen again."

She won't look at me as I'm led from the house. Her cries are following me down the stairs, and I want to tell her it's fine. Everything is warm and soft. I smile.

"In you go, Ella." Andrew opens the car door and I slide in. A bolt of fear shoots through me as the driver turns to me, but the feeling dies as quickly as it arrived.

"Mark," I say and he glances at Andrew.

"Drive." Andrew sits beside me, and I close my eyes. I want to go back to Lucas.

I smile again.

"Why are you smiling?" Andrew asks, and when I open my eyes, he's smiling at me.

"He gave me..." My tongue grows heavy, and his smile widens. "Typewriter," I manage to get out as I think of the small key ring.

The detail was fantastic. God, I have an amazing imagination.

I drift in and out of consciousness.

"Is that mess cleaned up?" Andrew's voice sounds different, and I want to look at him, but I can't move.

"They're doing it at the moment, Master Andrew."

"He's foolish. I have to explain to Matthew that his daughter is dead. I can't lose his investment."

My brain is scrambling, but it settles in a motel room, under the blankets. All I feel is Lucas's heavy arm around me as I fall asleep.

CHAPTER TWENTY-SIX

ELLA

My head hurts as I sit up. I have a moment of panic clawing at me. Lucas is all I can think about, and it's like the last few days flicker across my mind before it settles on Sandra bleeding to death and then Andrew helping me. A pool of sweat starts to dry up on my chest.

I look around me. I'm back in my room. The window is open and the curtains billow around the small reading table. It sounds like voices are melting together.

I reach the curtain as the bedroom door opens.

"Good morning, Ella." It's Andrew.

"Master Andrew," I greet him.

He smiles. "I'm glad to see you are feeling well."

"I think I would like some water please, Master Andrew." My throat feels dry. It's then I see the glass in his hand and I smile.

"Great minds think alike," he says as he steps up to me.

Fear snakes around my stomach, and I don't understand it. But my mind isn't right, and I have to try to separate the reality from what I made up.

He opens a hand, and a small white tablet sits in it. I hesitate. "Take it, Ella. It will keep you calm."

I pop it into my mouth and wash it down with the water.

"I have come with some news."

I bob my head.

"You broke some of the rules."

I nod my head again. I remember what I did. My face blazes with humiliation. "I'm sorry." Tears burn my eyes.

Andrew takes my face in his hands. "No sweet, Ella, you have no reason to be sorry." He smiles at me. "But you will still have to be punished."

I know I will. My stomach tightens, but the knot unravels itself quickly. "I will accept my punishment."

He releases my face. "Good."

He claps his hands three times, and two ladies arrive into my room with piles of red fabric in their arms.

"They will bathe and dress you. The gathering has started." His eyes flicker to the windows.

Are those all the voices I hear? The ladies start to get me ready and Andrew leaves.

There's something therapeutic in how they wash me. Once I'm back in the bedroom, they dry me, and I'm standing before them naked. But that's okay.

The red fabric is wrapped around my body. They keep wrapping, and I keep smiling, until there's only a red cloak left. They brush my hair and paint my face. Neither meet my eye, and that's okay. I decide I will go to my happy place.

His fingers entwine with mine. They're so much bigger. He's always so warm. His eyes bore into mine, and I swear I feel it caress my soul. My eyes spring open, and panic starts to claw at me as I step away from the ladies.

"Lucas." His name is filled with so much pain, but it dwindles.

It isn't real.

"I'm sorry." I want to tell them I'm broken, but neither ask for an explanation. The cloak is wrapped around me, and small black slippers are placed on my feet.

"Red Riding Hood." I was never fond of the fairy tale, but that's what I look like when I meet my eyes in the mirror.

"Yeah, let's take you to the wolf," one of the ladies says with a sneer.

"Imelda," the other lady corrects, and I have a moment of wondering if I heard her right. Both of them look at me with passive expressions, and I'm led from the room. I glance around the landing, expecting to see a group of girls but it's empty. We move downstairs, and I pause outside the drawing room.

"Can I have a minute?" I ask.

Imelda smiles at me. "Knock yourself out."

I open the door, and my hand trembles. I know what I want to see, but I remind myself it might not be here.

My throat tightens. It's here. The picture of Lucas. Wow. He's breathtaking. I walk to his picture, and all I want to do is feel his warmth, his flesh on mine. I reach out and touch him, but it's cold and rough under my hand.

A throat clears behind me, and Imelda is at the door. "We need to go."

I nod. How much time has passed with me standing here?

I'm taken under the house, and each time I look around me, triggers keep misfiring in my head.

I swallow the lump as I walk into a room guided by the two ladies.

My heart beats a bit faster as Andrew smiles at me. My eyes bounce to two people I know. Aine and Sean. Sean looks to Aine, and he wears an odd look, but Aine doesn't flinch at all. She still looks like she's smiling. My own lips tug up. There's a bald-headed man who watches me with fascination. He could be a doctor, and I suppose I would be a dream patient. The last man has me wanting to step back.

"This is who took my daughter's life?" He takes a step toward me, and I'm looking behind me. Shivers race up and down my arms at the sight of the empty space. I swing back around, and Andrew has placed a hand on the man who looks like he wants to hurt me.

"We aren't barbaric, Matthew. She will be punished. Just not by your hand."

The man called Matthew steps back with fire in his blue eyes. Eyes that are familiar.

"Sandra." I say her name, and he's in front of me.

Pain radiates from his eyes. "Why? She was a good girl."

"Why, what?" I'm afraid and as I look to Master Andrew, I find myself stepping closer to him. He accepts me with an open arm. I'm tucked close to him, and I feel better already.

"She's ill, Matthew. We've already discussed this."

Matthew frowns, but he doesn't follow me.

"I don't understand." I don't like how everyone is looking at me.

"Shh, it's okay." I feel a prick along my arm, and my body slumps, but Andrew holds me up.

"It's so warm." I giggle as I glance over at everyone. No one laughs with me.

"My daughter should never have been around someone so unstable." Matthew turns away from me, and Andrew's hold grows tighter. I'm sure my arms will bruise from his pressing fingers.

Bells ring. It's distant, but I hear them. "Wedding bells?" I say out loud.

No one answers me.

"Get the car." Andrew speaks to someone behind me.

Before turning to me, his eyes are dancing with excitement, and it jumps from him and onto me. "Where are we going?"

"To the gathering. Remember? I told you that you would be punished."

I'm nodding my head. That's right, he did. I like that I remember and that it's true.

"I won't accept anything less than a beheading." Matthew speaks loudly, and I know I must have heard him wrong. Andrew passes me over to Aine, who helps keep me upright.

She doesn't look at me.

"Don't forget who you're speaking to, Matthew. I won't be threatened."

"I only ask for what my daughter deserves, Master Andrew." There's a standoff between the two men.

"Tense," I say to Aine, and she doesn't laugh.

"But you will have her head," Andrew promises.

I swallow. Someone's going to lose their head.

"Off with her head," I sing. Everyone looks at me. "The queen in *Alice in Wonderland*." No one laughs.

Andrew reclaims my arm, and we start to walk. "Is this a play? Am I Red Riding Hood? Who's playing Alice?"

"So inquisitive." Andrew smiles at me and I like him. I think we will be friends.

We reach a car that is idling outside. The voices sound like thousands of people all talking at once.

"You, my dear, will be center stage."

My stomach twists with nerves.

"I'll be right with you," Andrew promises me, and I relax as I climb into the car. If he's with me, I'll be fine.

CHAPTER TWENTY-SEVEN

LUCAS (BEFORE)

The closer we get, the more my nerves jump. "Can you drive any faster?" I keep a hold on the overhead handle. I don't allow myself to think about her.

"We're nearly there." George's words have me looking at him. I hear the 'but' before he says it.

"You walking in there will do you no good. The first chance Master Andrew gets, you will be locked up."

"I don't care." I stare out the window while clenching my jaw, hoping that George stops.

"Lucas, you're thinking with your emotions. You have to let us help you."

I'm waiting for my mother to join George in his crusade of saving me, but she doesn't.

"You walk in there and it's over. It's over for you."

"I don't care," I repeat to George.

"It's over for all of us. It's over for Ella."

I cut a look at George, warning him, but he doesn't shy away. He keeps glancing from me to the road.

"You have to be smart about this, Lucas. Just for one moment, think. She's in your house. What will your father do?"

For the first time, I allow myself to think of what she could be doing right now.

"He won't kill her. He'll use her as bait," I say reluctantly. That alone has me tightening my fists.

"Exactly. I need to be the one going in there. No one will suspect me."

I release the handle and it bangs again. "I can't leave her." I feel so weak, and when I look at George, I see the understanding in his eyes.

"I've watched you grow from a little boy. Please trust me. I will get her. We just need to be smart."

What he's saying makes sense. My father would expect me to come for her, just like they would have expected her to go for Hannah and Jessie. The chances that she got out are slim, but that's a piece of hope I'm not releasing.

"Okay," I grind out.

George turns off the road after another fifteen minutes of silence. "Where are you going?"

He glances at me. "My home. I need to get changed and you can wait."

I'm already shaking my head. George takes another left, and we pull up to a modest-sized home. It makes him even more of a person. I never thought of him having a life outside of us.

"If I walk in there in normal clothes, it will trigger them. We need to be smart." He stops the car, and I hate getting out.

"Just give me a moment." George leaves me and my mother in a small sitting room together.

I know she's watching me, but she doesn't speak. I'm pacing the small space. My stomach twists and swirls. George arrives and he's dressed in his uniform for work.

"Aine said Hannah and Jessie were kept under the shed. Ella must have heard me and Aine talking the other night about it."

I was stupid to have questioned her about her strange behavior. The signs that she was up to no good were there, but I was too focused on hurting Alex rather than figuring out what was going on with her.

George nods. "I'll ring if I can, but otherwise just wait until I come back." He points at a black phone beside the TV. "Just stay by the phone."

"Be safe, George." My mother hugs him, and I look away.

Everything in me is saying this is wrong, but he's right. If I go in there, I can't just walk away. I'd be no good to Ella locked up, but that doesn't make this any easier.

The front door closes and the engine starts. I feel like a trapped animal. The room grows smaller, but all I can see is the black phone.

"Would you like a cup of coffee?"

"No." I can't even look at her. I want her away from me. I pull off the jumper; everything feels so tight. My mother leaves the room and I'm grateful.

I pick up the phone and check the tone. I tell myself he only just left. Replacing it, I try to distract myself by looking around the room. George has so many pictures. It surprises me how many there are of me and my mother.

I hear the rattle of ice and look to my mother as she holds out a glass to me. I take it and the liquid burns my throat.

"I don't remember these," I say, pointing at a picture with my glass. She sips her own brandy. There are so many pictures of us. One is us having a picnic with teddy bears. Another of us lying out under the trees. My eyes trail across one of George reading to me.

"You must have been four in that one." She points at one. I'm wearing tiny red shorts and a sky blue polo shirt. I'm laughing at the camera, and my mother is lying on a rug behind me, a sun hat covering her face. "You loved George so much. He was like a grandfather to you."

I glance at her and she's smiling at the image.

"You're close to him?"

She looks at me in surprise. "He's been the only person who didn't try to break me down. He was always rebuilding me." The sorrow in her eyes has me finishing my drink.

"Your father is clever. He will use her to get to you."

I don't want to talk about Ella. I step away from the shelving of snapshots of my childhood and continue my pacing. "How did you marry him?" I need to distract myself.

My mother shrugs. "It was the same process. Seven girls were presented, and I was the richest."

I'm picturing my mother as a young girl. I never thought of her like that before.

"Were you afraid?" Why am I asking these questions?

Once again, surprise flickers across her eyes. "No."

I sneer at that. Why did I think for one second she was fragile.

"I knew going in that I would be selected. I understood my role. I was raised to play the game."

"Of course you were." I don't want to listen to her anymore. I thought maybe I would find a trace of Ella in her; maybe she was afraid too. But no, she was as cunning as Sandra.

"I was raised like that, Lucas. You can't keep judging me. I did the best I could with what I knew."

I place the empty glass onto the fireplace.

"Your father was actually charming, and I fell for him very quickly."

"Spare me the details." I cut her off as I walk up to the black phone and stare at it. My will alone doesn't make it ring.

My mother leaves the room but arrives back with the bottle of brandy. She refills her glass, and I swipe the bottle from her and place it on top of the fireplace.

"Everyone needs to keep a clear head," I say.

She sips from the glass like I didn't just speak. She's staring at the TV.

"Will you hand me over to get her back?"

"It's crossed my mind," I lie.

Her eyes pinch at the corner, and I turn away from her. Time moves funny when you watch it. I'm ready to snap. I keep thinking of leaving the room, but each time I do, I fear the phone will ring.

"How long has he been gone?" My voice sounds dry. It is.

"It's been three hours." I hate how her brows draw down. She's worrying, and that isn't good.

"Something went wrong." I run my hands across my face. It's the hum of an engine that has me leaving the room.

"Stay by the phone," I bark at my mother as she tries to follow me. I open the front door, and George doesn't get to stop the car before I'm pulling the passenger door open. I can't see her; she's slumped in the seat.

Moving hair that's lighter than Ella's out of her face, each millisecond breaks me. It's Jessie. I don't think but place my arm under her legs and the other around her waist. I lift her from the car as George gets out.

His eyes meet mine, and he shakes his head. "She wasn't there."

I walk up to the house.

"Neither was Hannah." He closes the door behind me as I carry Jessie into the sitting room. Lying her out on the couch, I push more hair out of her face.

She's cold. I touch her neck and can feel a pulse. "What's wrong with her?"

"I think she's drugged." George places a blanket over her, but it won't take away every mark I can see on her body. He had his fun with her.

"We need to get to Hannah's home…"

George shakes his head. "I've already done that, Lucas. She never arrived home and neither did Ella. But they aren't there."

Relief has me taking a breath. Where would they go? And why did they leave Jessie behind?

"They wouldn't leave her behind." I point at Jessie now as my stomach tightens. I exhale loudly as I stare at Jessie. She might have answers.

"We need to wake her."

George removes his coat. "I've been trying. She won't wake up."

I reach for Jessie and shake her. She doesn't stir. I need answers. I shake her again, and her head rattles back and forth.

"Lucas, you'll hurt her." My hands burn, and I step away. My heart is pumping too hard. My mother scurries around me and rubs Jessie's face while retucking the blanket around her.

"We need to start looking."

"I don't think that's wise," George starts.

"I went along with you. I stayed here against all my instincts. I need to look for her."

Silence fills the room.

"I'm not asking, George." I don't want to fight with him, but if she's out there with Hannah, I need to find them.

"Elizabeth, you stay here with Jessie. Aine and the others should be here soon."

I grab the keys as George leaves instructions for my mother. I'm in the car and thinking of every place they could have gone. I have no ideas at all. She took Asher's Jeep. She could have returned to it with Hannah, and they could be anywhere by now.

George comes out of the house and gets into the car.

"Tell me every single detail." He does. Two broken doors, smashed glass, and Jessie—that's what he found under the shed. I keep looking at him, searching for any deception in his voice, but I don't find any.

"What about Henry?" I grind his name out.

George doesn't answer, and I glance at him. He scratches his neck before looking at me. "I can't find him either."

"You only decided to tell me that now?" I push my foot heavier on the peddle and watch the road waste away behind us. I have no idea where I'm running to. I just need to get somewhere fast. I grip the steering wheel.

"We don't know how long they've been missing, Lucas. They could be anywhere."

"I agree. That's why we need to start looking." I pull the Jeep over. We're a few kilometers from the house.

"We won't be the only one's looking for them."

I know that. That's why we need to find them first. I don't respond to George and get out.

Fields surround our house for miles. I know Ella lives in the vicinity.

"Do you have anyone else looking?" I ask George as I climb across a field gate.

George is slow getting across. "Yes, I have someone watching her house and Hannah's."

"Thank you, George," I say once his feet touch the grass, and we're walking across an open field. I have no idea where to start, but doing something makes me feel better than sitting in a room with my mother.

"I have friends looking for them, too."

I touch his shoulder as we walk. I hope he knows how grateful I am.

"They're on foot. Asher's Jeep is still parked at your house." I don't know if that makes this better or worse.

The more time that passes, the more pain explodes in my abdomen. Light's fading and fear is creeping out of the shadows.

George is exhausted. He's slowed down considerably. We're nearly back at the car.

"There are some old outhouses a few miles back. We should check them." George had checked in with his own people again, and neither Hannah nor Ella had arrived home.

"You need to go back to the house. We need to know if Henry—" My heart squeezes as George's phone rings. He's too fucking slow getting it out.

He answers and I'm staring at him. His eyes flicker up to mine, and I can see the ghost of a smile.

"They found Hannah."

I exhale on a smile, but it evaporates as George closes the phone and meets my eye.

"Only Hannah."

Trepidation drips like a broken tap into an already overflowing pool of fear.

CHAPTER TWENTY-EIGHT

LUCAS (BEFORE)

Hannah is awake when we arrive back to George's and I want to ask her a million questions. She's wrapped in a blanket. My mother is on her knees at Hannah's feet, trying to talk to her. Hannah's eyes slowly lift, and when they clash with mine, I see a spark of fear before they grow overwhelmed with guilt.

I can't even form words as I stare at Hannah.

"She rescued me and Jessie." Hannah looks over at Jessie, who's still lying unmoving. I don't even breathe as the guilt in Hannah's eyes grows deeper. "She told me to run." She blinks and tears fall.

"She told me to run," she repeats.

I don't move a muscle.

"I'm sorry." Hannah's outburst has my mother rubbing her leg, telling her it's okay.

"You left her," I finally say.

Hannah's face pales and her cries stop. She's shaking her head.

"Lucas."

I don't look at my mother. I won't allow Hannah to wallow.

"She was right behind me," Hannah says.

"Then where is she?"

Hannah's cries anger me. She left her. I left her.

"Henry has her," she finally admits. "He was chasing us, and Ella fought him and told me to run."

My chest tightens with pain.

Hannah sobs and my mother comforts her. I hear all the voices in the house now. The others must have arrived.

"We need to wake Jessie, to see if she can be more helpful." Hannah's cries stop again, but I refuse to look at her.

"Jessie hasn't been responsive since we've been down there," Hannah tells me, and I look at her in disgust from the corner of my eye. I have to leave the room before I hurt her.

"Lucas," my mother calls after me.

George is in the hall. All the color is bleached from his face. My body locks like it's preparing for a huge blow.

"Ella returned home." George's words sound good, but the delivery is devastating.

"Your father has already arrived, and he has her."

Aine and Sean step into the hall. "He's called a meeting." Aine speaks to me. "I'm betting it's about Ella. At least we can tell you what's happening."

My eyes skip across them all and land on Alex. He recoils and slithers back into the kitchen.

"When is the meeting?" I barely recognize my voice.

"In the morning." Worry mars Aine's plastic face.

I can't wait that long. They all see it.

"Can we have a minute?" George asks both Sean and Aine. Sean bobs his head, but Aine lingers. George, a servant having more control than she, isn't exactly something she's used to. Her eyes search mine, but she leaves, seemingly satisfied with what she sees.

"I know it's hard. But I will return and find out where she is. Through me, you will know how she is. We are so close." George grips both my arms, but I don't feel his hands on me.

"The gathering is tomorrow. Whatever your father has planned, will happen tomorrow. For now, we need to keep you safe."

I nod and George exhales loudly. "I'll get ready."

He leaves me and I close my eyes against the pain rising in me like a tide.

George's phone rings again, and I'm moving. He picks it up, and I don't look at Hannah, who my mother still clutches.

George flickers a glance at me. "Okay, okay. Where is he now? Okay. Thank you." He hangs up. "Sandra's body was found in a cell."

Sandra? What was she doing there?

"Henry is locked up now. That was your father's order," George finishes and my mother is standing.

Hannah continues to cry, and I want to tell her to shut up. I can't think with her wailing.

"So Henry killed her?"

"That's what I was just told," George confirms.

Henry.

"He was always cruel. I knew it would result in this." My mother's words bounce off me.

"I hope to have news soon." George leaves the room.

"Lucas." Hannah's voice has me glaring at her. She left her.

So did you, a voice says in the back of my head.

"I don't want to hear it," I bark, and she cries again as I leave the room.

"Don't do that to her. She has been traumatized." My mother is on my heels, and the hallway is growing smaller by the second.

"Get away from me," I warn her as I enter the kitchen. Asher, Sean, Aine, and Alex are all having a fucking tea party.

I'm ready to explode when a scream splits the air. My feet eat up the floor until I'm back in the sitting room. Jessie is awake and screaming.

"It's okay, Jessie. I'm here. It's Hannah." Hannah holds Jessie, and her screams are cut off.

I know she was asleep the whole time, but she might have something, one small detail that can make this more bearable.

"Did you see Ella?" I ask and the girls separate. Jessie looks up at me, and she's blinking rapidly. She peeks at Hannah before her attention turns back to me. "No. I don't remember." She looks around. "Where am I?"

Useless.

"Lucas," Hannah calls.

I can't look at her. She's a reminder of what I've done.

"Don't speak to me."

"She said she would be right behind me!" Hannah cries.

"Excuses. You left her to die!" The roar is torn from me. I know it's not her I'm angry with. It's myself.

"I'll do anything to fix this."

I see the damage and hurt in her eyes. I see each mark my brother inflicted on her. I'm leaving my own mark, and Ella would hate me for it.

I exhale loudly and look away from Hannah. Jessie is clutching the blanket in her whitened hands. They had been terrified enough. I'm aware of Asher at the door. No doubt ready to protect them.

"I'm sorry. This is my fault," I say to Hannah before I look at Jessie. "I'm sorry," I tell her and leave the room. I can't bear to keep looking at the results of my family's work.

***

George arrives back a time later. "She's safe." He's smiling, and I want to smile too but I can't. "Lucas, she's safe."

"My father still has her, so she isn't safe." *She's not here with me.* Only then will I relax. I scrub a hand across my face.

George ignores me and joins me on the steps at the front of his house. I can't go back in. I can't bear to be around anyone. I feel so useless.

"She's in her room, asleep. I think your father suspects me."

I glance at George now. "Why?"

"It's more of a feeling. I left early."

I'm thinking about her asleep in her bed, and it's just not adding up. "He must have her drugged, like the way Jessie was. There's no way she would sleep," I say.

"Tomorrow you will have her back, and all this will be over."

Tomorrow may as well be a million years away.

"We all need to rest. We only have a few hours left."

I want to go now. I want to climb into her room and take her. But I know it won't be that simple. I know he'll have her guarded. The only time I can really get to her is at the gathering. It's my only chance.

***

I don't sleep even as my body demands it. Aine and Sean have left for the meeting, and I can't stay still.

"Anything?" I ask George for the thousandth time. He doesn't answer me, but I can see I'm grating on his nerves. The room keeps growing smaller and smaller each time I look at the clock. The gathering is taking place soon.

The door opens and my mother nods at us. Her words don't leave her mouth quick enough. "It's confirmed. She's on her way to the gathering."

I brush past my mother, and Asher blocks the door. "Remember, you need to do as we planned. Rushing in there will result in failure."

"I agree." I don't turn to Hannah, who's suited and booted like she's going to war. I also don't look at her because she's so different this morning. She's harder around the edges, and I can see the want in her to draw blood.

I want that fire in her so she'll stop at nothing to get Ella back. I had promised myself I wouldn't think of Ella, but my mind never left her.

"What are we waiting for?" I call out to George. Asher still hasn't left the front door. My heart races.

"We're ready." George and my mother follow us out the door. Asher, Alex, and Jessie take Sean's car. He went with Aine. Hannah and my mother climb into the back. I drive and once George is in, I'm reversing out the driveway.

***

"How many people do you think are here?" I'm as stunned as Asher. Tens of thousands of people move around the field. Stalls have been set up with food and drinks. A huge stage far off is our destination. The crowd is broken up into smaller groups of people talking. Some are drinking and dancing. I see the more elite members have small VIP tents they've gathered under. I move through a cloud of cigar smoke.

"You need to blend in more, Lucas," Asher hisses at me. I'm plowing through people. I'm so close and I don't want to mess it up, so I slow my pace as I move through the crowd.

Each step is a step closer. My heart pounds so fast as I see movement on the stage. Someone is setting out a row of chairs. I can't make the person out. I'm still too far away.

Screens on either side are still in darkness. Speakers are set up everywhere.

Fear clutches me as the speakers screech and the screens turn on. People around me cover their ears until the sound settles. I can't look away from the two black limos pulling up around the back of the stage. There's excitement among the crowd as the doors open on the second car. Aine, Sean, Brendan, and Cathal climb out, along with Matthew Crowley. The crowd applauds, and it reminds me how recognizable we are. I tug on my cap, pulling it low over my eyes. They climb the steps at the side of the stage.

I start to move again through the crowd. The roar ripples across the people, causing the hairs on my arms to rise as my father climbs out of the first car. He's their God. They are his followers.

The cheers don't cease. He stands at the car door and waves, soaking up their applause. My heart stalls as he turns and reaches out his hand. I see a flash of red. It grows until the hooded figure is standing beside him. She faces the camera, and I'm staring into green eyes that set me on fire.

Ella.

CHAPTER TWENTY-NINE

ELLA

There are so many people. Their cheers ring out around me, and I'm staring at Andrew in wonder. This is for him. They love him. These are his people. My mind tries to piece together why I'm here, but it disintegrates as the roars take over.

"They love you," I tell him.

His eyes move to me, and he smiles. Taking my chin in his hands, he holds my face. His touch is gentle. "They love you."

I frown. "Why?"

His chuckle has him releasing me. "You are the main attraction." He closes the door behind me and holds out his arm for me to take.

I'm nervous at each step we climb. I'm a little starstruck as we clear the last step, and the roar of people have my soul lifting. Fear clutches me, but Andrew squeezes my hand that's wrapped around his arm.

"You have nothing to fear." His reassurance has me stepping forward with him. He leads me to a chair that's right beside Aine. Helping me sit down, he takes my hand and plants a kiss on it. I can't stop the smile as I shyly duck my head.

He releases me, and the crowd's cheers grow wilder. I want to cry. The feeling is overwhelming, to think of so many people in one place at once. I've never seen so many. The ones further away are dots. Why are they here? I remember the play. I look down the line, and I can't for the life of me fathom what everyone else is playing.

"What are you playing?" I can't figure out her character. I'm thinking of someone evil. Her eyes grow wide, and she stares at me. Definitely someone evil. She would be very good, I decide.

I refocus my attention on Andrew. It's hard to keep my eyes off him. He keeps drawing me in. Even with his back to me, he still commands me and the surrounding space. I look out into the crowd, where each face is focused on him.

Large screens blow him up, and I freeze when I see myself on the large screen. It's my face. I raise my hand and touch my cheek. Is this real? Something tugs at me, but it vanishes just as quickly. I tilt my head, and so does the girl on the screen. I hear laughter at the front of the stage, and the image skips over to the rest of the lineup. None of them stare at the camera. I shouldn't stare at the camera.

"Welcome, ladies and gentlemen." Andrew's voice booms, and I look at the line of people I'm beside. Everyone is focused on Andrew except Matthew, who glares at me.

I frown at him before sitting back in my seat. His hostility is confusing and unwarranted. Bile rises in my throat as an image of a blonde-haired girl in a pool of blood fills my mind. Oh God. I'm having another episode.

"It's been fifty years since we last gathered. Look at how we've grown." More applause rings out, and I think I should clap too.

I keep my focus on Andrew. He really is a formidable force. This would have been so daunting, coming up on stage, but with his presenc, I felt like I could do this.

"Today marks so much." The crowd quiets. "Today, I want to tell my people how proud I am. Look at our growth." More clapping erupts.

"But, with growth comes weeds. And weeds must be pulled."

I nod. That is very true. Weeds can really be pesky things when left untreated.

"We have something so beautiful here." Andrew turns and looks at the line of us. His eyes linger on me. "But it is spoiled with weeds that we will pluck from the root." He turns back to the crowd.

"With a heavy heart"—he covers his heart with his hand—"I'm reporting two people for treason." There is a lull in the noise of the crowd, and I'm on the edge of my seat.

"Aine and Sean have conspired to take my throne." Some people boo, and I can't look away from Aine.

Her face grows ghastly as a group of men step up to her. She rises and so does Sean. I had liked them. They seemed nice.

A memory of Aine in a cabin claims me, and my hand shoots out to her. She stops and looks down at me. I don't understand the fear that's clinging to me like a second skin.

She's taken from me, along with Sean. I can't tear my eyes off them.

"They will face the penalty for treason..." He waits until everyone falls silent. "Death."

My stomach twists and settles a millisecond later.

Both of them are taken off the stage. Aine struggles and looks back at me. She's shouting something, and I shake my head at her. I can't hear what she's saying. She disappears and I sit forward. There's a gap between Matthew and I—two empty seats. His eyes bore into me, and I shift uncomfortably.

"The next matter is one I do with a very heavy heart."

Someone close to the front of the stage catches my eye. He has a cap pulled down over his eyes, but I feel the full impact of his stare. My eyes burn and I look at Andrew. What's wrong with me? I remember I'm sick, but he's going to fix me.

The stranger moves again, and I find him easily in the crowd. His build fits perfectly with the one I made up. The one who danced with me in the snow. I'm back there dancing in circles as the snow melts under our feet. Pain tears through me, and I'm standing. I want to see his eyes. I want to call him out and demand that he show me his face.

"A young life was taken viciously, and the act was one that cannot be overlooked." Andrew peeks at me and smiles. I'm looking at him while trying to find the stranger in the crowd. I can't see him.

His voice haunts me.

"I won't lie, this is by far one of the hardest decisions I have ever made. But I will not forsake our rules for my own selfish ventures."

Where is he? I'm scanning the crowd, and now a silence falls. When I look up, I see Andrew is staring at Matthew, who is also standing. I have no idea what's going on.

"Matthew Crowley, you have committed the murder of Sandra Crowley, and in doing so, you will face your punishment."

Matthew turns to me, his face tightening. He disappears from my sight as men circle him.

"The punishment for taking a life is death."

A roar goes up, and I can't look away as Matthew is taken off the stage. He's trying to break free from the formation of men. He isn't screaming at Andrew. He's pointing at me. He's calling me a murderer. I can't hear him, but I can read the words on his lips that he keeps repeating.

Once he disappears, I sit back down. That are a lot of people dying today. *Now there were three* rings in my head.

The crowd settles and Andrew finds my eyes again and smiles. "Now since all the messiness is out of the way, let's have some good news. Can you all please welcome my son, the heir to the throne, your next leader, Henry O'Faolain?"

The crowd goes wild, and I'm feeling their excitement as I look toward the steps that lead up onto the stage. I see his dark hair, then dark eyes. He's tall and handsome in a red military jacket. His eyes meet mine, and something in me recoils. He doesn't look away from me—there's a predatory hunger in his eyes. I'm expecting him to walk past me, but he doesn't. He leans in and I try to hold still as he brushes a kiss across my cheek.

"Red is my favorite color," he sings.

"Black is my favorite color," another voice says.

I'm searching for the owner of the voice in the crowd again, but he isn't real. My heart pangs, and I look up into Henry's face.

"I told you I could convince him to let me have you as my wife." His words are whispered in my ear before he stands up and waves out at his adoring fans. He's handsome as he steps up to his father.

"Thank you all so much. What a wonderful welcome." Henry's voice is clear and precise. "Today, I want to share a gift with every one of you. You all have a front-row seat to my wedding!"

There are cheers, and Henry looks back at me. I don't understand.

Andrew comes to me and helps me rise. "This is your big moment. You are going to marry Henry."

"I thought I was little Red Riding Hood." I'm so nervous.

Andrew takes my face in his hands. "A change of plans. But you can do this."

He believes in me so much. A priest steps up onto the stage. He looks the part. "Should I not be in white?" I ask Andrew.

"You are stunning in red." He kisses both of my cheeks and leads me over to Henry. My feet are acting funny. It's like they're trying to walk in the opposite direction.

Henry smiles at me, and before I can gather myself, his lips touch mine. His lips are warm and soft, but everything in me screams. I don't understand my reaction to him. He breaks the kiss and smiles at me. My smile wobbles. Andrew removes the mic from the stand.

"Now, now, wait until you are declared husband and wife." A laugh sings out from the crowd, and I can feel the burn on my cheeks. Henry laughs, and the image flashes to him laughing in a cell. Fear claims me, and I'm frozen. But I blink and it all ceases. The fear dissipates.

The priest takes his place in front of us. He has a real Bible in his hands. I look around me and my stomach twists. The boy with the cap is at the stage again, only this time I can see his eyes. Eyes that bore into mine. Eyes that call to me. Eyes that are breaking me.

I know you. I know you. Something in me is clawing and fighting. He moves around, and I follow his movements. He's climbing the steps and I face forward.

Andrew is talking to the priest, and I pull on his sleeve. Sweat is making a pathway down my back. I glance at Lucas as he steps up onto the stage. I'm having another episode. I remind myself I'm the only one who can see him. He is everything and more. His eyes are the depths of the deepest ocean. He's a little scarier right now than I remember.

"Does anyone have any objections before we start?" The priest speaks into the mic, and I can't look away from the illusion.

I want to walk over and touch his face. My throat contracts painfully. He's too beautiful. I should have known he wasn't real.

"I object."

I startle at his voice, and now I know it's time for me to knock it off. Everyone will see how crazy I am. Andrew will regret giving me this role.

Why am I in a play? The question zooms past me, and my hands sweat. Andrew's head snaps up at the sound of Lucas's voice, and I know I must have spoken out loud.

Henry's face grows stiff, and I know I've really messed up.

"Ella."

I can't look at Lucas. He's calling my name. Oh God. Maybe if I keep facing forward, the image will dissolve. The only thing that isn't right is that it seems like Andrew and Henry can see him too. But that's not possible.

CHAPTER THIRTY

LUCAS

She's looking at me like I'm a stranger. The plan we talked about flies away, and my lungs contract painfully. She's leaning toward my father like she's afraid of me. The fear of her forgetting me on the stage in front of the world is growing and forming, and I'm freezing.

Ella steps away from my father and pushes the hood down. She's bewitching with her beauty. Each step she takes has my heart pumping. She's here, and she is safe. I want to grab her and pull her into my arms. Only then can I finally breathe.

She reaches me and her smell circles around me. I inhale deeply. Her hand rises, and I'm craving her touch. Her finger jabs my chest, her eyes growing wide, and she jumps back. Tears fill her eyes, but they don't spill as she turns away from me before looking back at me.

She swallows.

"Ella." I reach for her, and she steps away from me.

"Ella, sweetheart." My father's voice has the blood turning cold in my veins. My heart freezes when Ella steps to him. I look up to see the world watching us. They can't hear us, but we're filling their screens. My eyes flicker to Henry, and he smiles at me.

"Don't get sour," he says. "The best man won."

I compose myself and remember who I am. Asher was circled by a group of men only a few moments before I came on stage, so it confirmed our suspicions that my father knew we were all together. Maybe

Ella told him; maybe someone betrayed us. Either way, someone told him. Ella hasn't taken her eyes off me.

I take a step toward them.

"I have your mother locked up. Your plan of bringing Asher in as a witness is gone." My father speaks before turning to the crowd and smiling as if to assure them that my presence was planned.

I nod. "I have something I would like to say." I open my hand for the mic, and Ella stares at it like it's a gun. What did they do to her? I don't let that thought fully soak in. I'm barely keeping it together.

"Why do you want to tarnish me?" my father sneers. I take another step and hate how panicky Ella looks.

I glance at her and see the pulse in her neck beating rapidly.

"Are you afraid?" I question my father, and his eyes tighten. He won't harm me with the world watching.

"You have nothing on me." His confidence has him smiling.

"I know." He took all that away.

He grins and steps up to me. It's quick when he pulls me into his side. "Let's give these people a show, and then I shall deal with you."

His words are delivered to plant fear in me, but all I want to do is hurt him.

He looks up into the crowd and raises the mic to his lips. "Today is truly full of surprises. My youngest, Lucas O'Faolain."

Cheers ring out, and I see myself on the screen, but to my left is Ella. She's looking at me like her heart is breaking. I turn and our eyes clash. *I love you.* I hope she can see it in my eyes.

I take the mic from my father's hands, and he releases it with such confidence. If I go against him, he'll have me locked up. These people see him as their leader. My word against my father will mean nothing. I never understood the true power of the position he held until now.

"It's an honor to be here. I want to first congratulate my brother on his upcoming wedding." I look to Henry, and he steps closer to Ella, wrapping an arm around her waist. I allow myself to picture breaking each finger before turning back to the crowd.

I smile. "So perfect. I won't hold up the ceremony too long. I just wanted to use this opportunity to tie up a loose end for my father." I point at him, and his smile looks like he's intrigued, but I see the warning in his eyes.

"My father left me with a task to find the person responsible for one of the committee member's death." A hush falls around the crowd. Maybe the'are trying to think of who died recently. "It took me a while, but I finally figured it out." I glance down at the sea of smiling faces. A guy in the front row gives me an encouraging thumbs up.

"Hurry up," Henry hisses.

I laugh. "He's getting impatient." A few join my laughter. "I won't keep my brother waiting. So please bring the accused up," I call and face the side of the stage. My heart is pounding as blond hair is the first piece I see.

Alex is dragged across the stage by two men. "Ladies and gentlemen, the man responsible for the death of the committee member, Alex Bradley. His sentence will be death." The crowd roars, and Henry stumbles across the stage.

"He didn't do it," Henry barks at me, his control slipping so easily.

"Henry, control yourself." My father steps up to Henry, and I see Ella between the two figures. She's just staring at me.

"Remember me," I mouth to her.

Her eyes waver and she blinks. Tears spill down her face.

"He didn't do it." Henry is growing more frantic, and I need to finish this.

"Henry…" Alex doesn't say any more, but the fear is real in his eyes. I turn to Alex, and his eyes meet mine. He told me he would do anything it took to make this right, and this is what it will take. I nod at him.

"I killed Declan. I was jealous." Alex speaks into the mic I hold out to him. It won't mean anything to them. It will be just another person being sentenced to death. It's only entertainment to them. To Henry, it's everything. It's confirmation that Alex loves him.

Henry does it beautifully as he marches up to my father.

"Father, stop this right now."

"I can't," my father growls at Henry, then smiles up at the screens once again trying to reassure his people it's under control.

"Henry, the ceremony." Father smiles at him and reaches for Henry, but he pulls himself away.

"You killed Declan." He points at my father. "He will not die for this." Henry's eyes grow wilder, and he stands in front of Alex, and he's the turncoat I knew he would be.

They used Ella's love on me, so I would use Henry's love for Alex on him.

"Henry, this is what Lucas wants. He's forcing your hand. He's trying to take your place." My father's patience is running out, and I know I need to get Ella out of the line of fire.

Henry narrows his eyes at me. "I swear it's yours. I don't want to lead. He gave me the power to punish the person responsible and that person is Alex."

"Why are you saying you did it?" Henry pleads with Alex, and for the first time, I think I see the same care in Alex's eyes for Henry too.

"I hated seeing you with him." Alex does it beautifully.

Henry shakes his head.

I look to the last committee members. "He gave me that power and I'm only using it."

Brendan nods. "That is your right."

"No. Alex didn't do it. Father flipped the switch because Declan loved me." Henry is growing more frantic, and it's my father that realizes the crowd has grown deadly quiet. I've kept the mic on, and they're hearing each and every word.

"Alex will not die. I am your leader." Henry screams out into the crowd. The screens go blank, and I know it's time to get Ella off the stage.

My father tightens his fists. "If you don't shut up, Henry..."

When it comes to Alex, Henry can't control himself. He walks over to me and takes the mic, standing taller. He covers it first and composes himself.

"I will sort this out," he tells Alex as he addresses the crowd.

"Alex Bradley is an innocent man."

Across the stage, my father sees his time is running out, but so is mine. I step around them, and Ella flinches again. Reaching into my pocket, I take out the key ring I got her.

"Release him now." I glance at Henry, who turns to the two men who hold Alex. They don't release Alex, and Henry stamps over to them.

I focus on Ella and take her hand while pressing the key ring into it. When her eyes flicker up to me, I can't stop myself. I take her face in my hands and press my lips to hers. The screech of the microphone bangs like thunder before the noise is gone and the crowd all erupts at once. George has cut off all power.

I lean out and look into Ella's eyes. "I love you."

"Lucas." She reaches up a shaky hand and touches my face.

"Stop this right now." Henry is marching back up to my father, who looks to me with a smile. "Very clever, Lucas."

I keep Ella behind me as I face my father and Henry.

"Announce to the people that me and Ella are pardoned and this ends now," I tell him.

This is it. It's our only way out. I can't spend the rest of my life running. I clutch the mic in my hand.

"Tell me yes and the power will be turned back on. You make the announcement and me and Ella leave. You have my word that you won't see me again."

"Give him what he wants." Henry looks ready to explode.

"Sodomy is a crime that is punishable by death. If you don't mind your tongue, I'll have you hung."

Henry grows still at my father's angry words.

"Henry…" Alex pleads again, and Henry looks torn.

"He killed your mother, Sorcha," Henry. "He killed Declan, and now Alex will die for his crimes."

Brendan and Cathal stand. "Is there any truth in this?"

"Yes, he did it," Henry shouts at them, jabbing his finger in my father's direction. "He killed all those people, not Alex. Him." Henry dances away from my father as he glares at him.

I raise a fist in the air, and within seconds, the screens come back on, along with the sound. The crowd cheers, waiting for their wedding. My father glares at me, knowing he's in a corner, and there's only one way out.

"Make the announcement." I hold out the mic to him, and he takes it.

"Maybe we can renegotiate," he starts, fighting to control this situation.

"Pardon us now."

Anger tightens his jaw, and my father looks out on the people and smiles, but the strain is evident on his face.

"Ladies and gentlemen." He looks at me. "A pardon has been granted to Ella O'Leary and Lucas O'Faolain. Any charges have been dropped." Some people clap, but I can see no one has a clue what is going on.

But his word is final and said in front of everyone.

"What about Alex?" Henry is racing toward my father.

My father covers the mic. "I will deal with it in a minute."

I entwine my fingers with Ella and move to the back of the stage.

"You aren't going until Alex is freed." Henry follows behind me, but I don't stop.

I keep dragging Ella with me. I just want her off the stage and somewhere safe.

A gunshot has the crowd erupting in screams. I throw Ella down and cover her as I look around me. Henry is standing in the middle of the stage with a gun in his hand. What is he doing with a gun?

"Now. You listen to me. You aren't going anywhere until Alex is free." Henry fires a second shot into the air, and the crowd stampedes across each other. My father's face grows whiter by the second. This will be a gathering the people will never forget.

"You know there's only one way to free him," I grit out through my teeth. I hate how he's waving the gun around.

"I will lift it." My father takes a step but freezes as Henry points the gun at him.

"You will admit to killing Declan?"

Brendan and Cathal are frozen in their chairs. I see the priest hiding under the podium, clutching the Bible. I reach around me and touch Ella, hoping she finds comfort in me.

"You know he did all this to us." My father lowers his voice and tries to manipulate Henry, but he has no understanding of what Alex means to him.

The men holding Alex look unsure, and I know if they get the opportunity, they'll run.

"Fine. Just put the gun down." Henry starts to lower it. It's slow and my father moves quickly. He takes Henry to the ground fast, and a third shot rings out.

CHAPTER THIRTY-ONE

ELLA

My hands rest on his back. I'd gladly stay here forever. He's so warm. His hand moves around and touches my arm. I place my hand over his. I'm aware of how much larger his fingers are compared to mine. I remember the feel of them on my flesh. My body jerks as a gun is fired for the third time. His heart jumps, and for one second, I fear something has happened to him.

"Lucas." I'm pulling at him, trying to make him look at me.

He's rising and pulls me with him fast. My eyes are drawn to the blood that pools out around Henry and Andrew.

Lucas shoves me behind him, but I can't look away from the growing pool of blood. Henry is trapped under Andrew, but he pushes him off. Andrew hits the stage, blood bubbling from his mouth as he coughs.

I see Sandra bleeding out in the cell as Henry repeatedly stabs her. Bile claws its way up my throat.

"Now say it! Tell them!" Henry roars as he climbs on top of his father and grips his suit jacket. He shakes him. "Tell them!"

"Henry." Lucas's voice rattles through the hand I've kept pressed to his back. "He's dying." Pain radiates from Lucas's voice.

"Tell them you did it. Tell them you killed Declan." Henry doesn't hear Lucas as he continues to shake Andrew violently. Andrew's head flops back and forth with the force.

Movement to my left catches my attention. The last two committee members are trying to sneak off stage.

Henry drops Andrew with a heavy thud and reclaims his gun. His hands are covered in blood. There's so much blood.

"Don't move." Both of the members freeze. Henry wipes sweat off his face with his sleeve.

"You have to listen to his confession."

"Ella." I can hear a hiss to the right of the stage.

Hannah smiles at me and waves me down. "Come on." Her eyes are wide as she lies on the steps.

"Tell them what you did!" Henry's roars have me jumping.

"Ella, go to Hannah." Lucas's voice is low, and he releases me from his hold, but I can't step away from him.

I don't move and Hannah hisses. My chest tightens.

"Ella, go! Please," Lucas begs and I release his back. The horror of losing him has me freezing.

"I killed…" Andrew speaks, blood gargling from his mouth. Henry's eyes are wide and wild as he holds him up by the jacket. The gun is still clutched in his hand.

Lucas grips my wrist, and I look up at him. "Go," he mouths and I hear it all, all the missing words crammed into that one word. All my memories are real. The confirmation has me spinning.

"Ella," Hannah hisses again. Hannah. *Ella, who isn't Bella.*

I close my eyes as I slip away. The moment my feet touch the step, Hannah is standing and grabbing me around the waist. Jessie holds out her hand, waiting for me. Another shot is fired, and Hannah pulls me down along with her.

"Lucas." I'm scrambling back up. "Lucas." Horror rushes throughout my system and crushes my heart. "Lucas."

"No." Hannah drags me back, and Jessie grips my arm. They're pulling me away from the stage. Away from Lucas.

"Lucas!" I scream again. I can't see what's happening. I can't lose him.

My eyes dart to the screen, and he's standing like an avenging angel. There's no fear in his eyes. Jessie and Hannah continue to pull me, and I'm getting glimpses of him as I glance over my shoulder.

He's beautiful and frightening all at once, and I'm so drawn in. We are moving toward a car. I glance back to see one of the committee members bleeding out on the stage. That's who was shot. Relief that it isn't Lucas is short-lived as I watch Henry waving the gun around, but I can't hear what he's saying.

Lucas holds my attention. There's something so feral in the smile he gives Henry before it shatters, and he throws himself at Henry.

A scream is lodged in my throat as Hannah and Jessie drag me into a car.

"Lucas!"

"Will be fine. This is what he wanted." Hannah's soft green eyes hold mine. And I'm clambering for the door.

"Drive, George." The car hums under us, and I'm shaking my head, clawing for the door. "I can't leave him."

The car moves. "This is what he wanted." Hannah holds me, and I push her away. "I can't lose him again." Tears blur my eyes.

"We can't lose you either."

I plaster myself against the window as the stage grows smaller behind me. "Lucas," I whisper.

"Shh." Hannah pulls me back and holds me. "I'm so sorry." Her cries join mine. "I shouldn't have left you."

Jessie wraps her arms around me too and her own cries join mine.

My stomach is twisted in knots when George pulls up outside a farmhouse. I'm out of the car, and I can't stand still.

"He said to bring you here." George gets out and walks over to me. "He will come here the minute he can."

I'm shaking my head. "I didn't think he was real."

George's eyes fill with pity.

"Come inside." Hannah wraps an arm around my waist.

I don't want to go in. I want to wait for him.

"He won't be long," Hannah promises, and I let her lead me in. There's something different about her and Jessie. It's in their eyes. They've seen too much.

George pours us out a drink and hands each of us a glass of brown liquid. I smell it and I'm standing at a bar with Lucas, right after Declan's wake. My head bows with the weight of the memory. I don't want anyone to see me. "I need air."

Hannah steps up to me.

"Alone. Please."

"Every time you leave my sight, bad things happen." Jessie reaches Hannah and the look of understanding in her eyes toward Hannah makes me see the strain I've put on both of my friends.

"What's going to happen in a garden?" I ask, faking nonchalance and taking a drink from the glass. It burns and I like how it feels.

Hannah half laughs. "With you anything is possible." Her smile touches her eyes, and I see my friend in them.

"I need to wait for him," I say and she nods. I remove the heavy red cloak and leave it on the banister in the hall. Standing outside, I finish my drink. I think of getting into the car and driving back, but I've made so many reckless decisions that have endangered the people I love. I lower myself and sit on the step. I would wait. No matter how long it took.

My eyes burn from not blinking, but I don't want to miss a thing. I feel my time was stripped from me, and I don't want it to disappear. I sit until the sound of a vehicle has me standing up. I tell myself to breathe. I reach out and touch the wall. I press my hand into the stone. I'm here. This is real, I tell myself as a black car pulls up. The engine turns off, and I can't breathe as Lucas gets out.

"Lucas." My voice wavers, and he couldn't possibly hear me. I'm off the steps and moving. He meets me halfway, and I don't pause as I throw myself into his open arms. His arms tighten around me, and I let my hands roam across his shoulders and chest. He's here. He's alive. A sob of laughter pulls from me as I touch his face.

"Lucas," I again and when his lip tugs up, something inside burns brightly.

"It's over," he tells me, his hands tightening on me again. "No one will ever hurt you again."

His words are followed by the press of his lips against mine. He doesn't close his eyes and neither do I. I'm afraid if I blink, he will disappear.

"I love you." The words wind themselves around our joined lips and sink deep inside me.

I blink and he's still here. My hands sink into his hair as I pull him closer and deepen the kiss. Close isn't close enough. There's not *enough* with Lucas; he will never run out, an endless supply of perfection. But fear makes me greedy, and I pull him closer, my fingers running rapidly across his face, tracing the perfection that makes him up.

A throat is cleared, and I'm happy enough to ignore it. Lucas laughs gently into our kiss. He keeps me in his arms.

"Thank you." He speaks with all his heart, and I look around to see George on the doorstep.

"It's done. It's over," Lucas tells George. He detangles us but entwines my fingers with his. It's not enough for me. I want him alone, where I can claim him.

"Your father?" George asks.

"Is dead. Henry shot him." We take a step toward George.

"Henry?" George asks and I stiffen as the cloak that blocked my emotions lifts with each passing minute.

Lucas shakes his head. "I had no choice. He killed Cathal and was ready to kill Brendan so there would be no committee and he could lead with Alex."

Alex! Oh God. Is he okay?

"You did what any leader would have done." George reaches out and places a hand on Lucas's shoulder.

"Everyone is back at the house. I told them we would join them tomorrow." His hand tightens around my fingers, and I'm so grateful.

George looks relieved as he exhales on a smile. "It's over."

"It's over, George."

***

We don't join anyone the next day. Lucas stays in the cocoon we create in a double bed in George's house. I don't ever want to leave it. I'm holding my key ring, shaking it from left to right like a pendulum. Lucas watches me with a smile on his lips I can't get enough of. The morning light is shining through a crack in the curtains and shedding light across half his face.

"I love you, Ella." His words are filled with an ache I hope will never be filled.

"If that's true..." I tighten my hand around the key ring and smile up at him. "You will stay here with me forever."

His lips tug higher, and my heart flips. "That's a very enticing proposition." He pulls me closer to him, and I willingly go. His shaft grows hard again. "How about we stay here for a while longer?" He opens my hand and entwines our fingers. His eyes lock on the key ring.

"I really like the sound of that."

His eyes darken with a hunger I'm ready to feed.

"I wish Ella O'Leary would marry me."

My heart feels like it's ready to explode in my chest. His dark eyes are so light. and I watch the gold flecks swirl and dance.

"I wish Ella O'Leary would marry me," I echo back, and his smile would conquer nations and stop wars.

He is everything.

He is mine.

EPILOGUE

LUCAS

I can't take my eyes off Ella as she smiles from Hannah to Jessie. They group together as I flip another burger.

"We make a great team."

I flick a glance at Alex and smirk at him. "I wouldn't go that far."

He sips from his bottle as he looks at the committee members. He's nervous and his eyes still look haunted after all that transpired.

"Thank you for agreeing to this," I say while flipping the burger again. I never personally barbequed before, but this experience was a first for Ella. She had seen it on TV and thought it looked fun. She looks up at me as if she can feel my eyes on her. Her green eyes sparkle, and I know how lucky I am.

"Honestly, I had nothing better to do."

I laugh at Alex, and he steps away and joins his father at the table. He's now part of the committee.

"Shall I take over so everything isn't burned?" George arrives and I'm quick to hand him the tongs.

I don't meet my mother's eyes as she seeks me out. She refocuses on Aine and Sean, but I catch the sadness in her eyes. I get it, but I'm not ready yet.

I pull Ella close to me and kiss her gently. "I can barely concentrate when you keep looking at me," I tell her.

She laughs and so does Hannah. "I did nothing." Her smile is wide.

I kiss her again. "You're here, so that's distracting."

"Shall I leave?" She pretends to walk away.

I pull her back. "Never."

She exhales loudly and leans into me.

"I'd tell you to get a room, only you would, and we wouldn't see you again," Hannah teases and Ella sticks out her small pink tongue at her.

My mind goes south and I drag it back.

I meet Ella's mother's eye. She's seated with the committee members. She's only here because she's Ella's mother. Otherwise, she would never be in my company. I will never forgive her for giving up on Ella.

"Do you want to tell everyone?" I ask Ella, and her smile is nervous.

"You tell them." She doesn't like public speaking.

I turn her toward everyone.

"We have an announcement to make."

Aine raises a brow, and I can see it on her and my mother's face: *Don't tell us she's pregnant.*

"The twenty-seventh of February. Save the date."

"The wedding?" Ella's mother can barely breathe as she joins her hands together in prayer.

"Yes, I'm getting married." Everything is worth it to see the pure joy on Ella's face right now.

She bites her bottom lip as she looks up into my eyes. "*We* are getting married."

I hold her face and kiss her, and everyone cheers.

"To Ella and Lucas!" Brendan says.

I release Ella as everyone rises with their drinks. I nod at Brendan. I hadn't expected him to stay, but he did.

"To Ella and Lucas," everyone repeats before drinking.

We have a community to rebuild. The chaos that followed after my father and Henry's deaths was hard to control, but we managed to restore some faith into the community.

My mother had taken the position as leader, not me. I'm not ready yet. I'm on the committee, but I'm not leading. I want time with Ella. We have so many first things to make come true for her, and I plann to make sure I don't miss a second of her experiencing life with me.

I hold her tighter. This is our beginning. She turned out to be my savior.

My everything.

THE END

WHY NOT TRY OUT "DECEIVE ME" BY VI CARTER. A NEW ADULT COLLEGE ROMANCE HERE

About The Author

When Vi Carter isn't writing contemporary & dark romance books, that feature the mafia, are filled with suspense, and take you on a fast paced ride, you can find her reading her favorite authors, baking, taking photos or watching Netflix.

Married with three children, Vi divides her time between motherhood and all the other hats she wears as an Author.

She has declared herself a coffee & chocolate addict! Do not judge

Social Media Links for Vi Carter

Website

Facebook Reading Group

Facebook Author Page

www.ingramcontent.com/pod-product-compliance
Lightning Source LLC
Chambersburg PA
CBHW030749190726
48285CB00003B/774